STOLEN ICE BRIDE

STOLEN BRIDES OF THE FAE

ANGELA J. FORD

enjoy this
icy adventure

CHAPTER 1

The air was heavy with apprehension. I tasted it on my tongue as I worked, grinding the herbs into a fine powder. My nerves were raw with worry. I should have left the eve before, for when spring breaks the unforgiving grip of winter, the mages arrive to steal a bride.

It was the morning of the tithe required by the mages who ruled Lansing Falls, a scattering of villages perched on the great lake in the northern reaches of the empire of Nomadia. In exchange for a tithe, the mages offered protection from the ice lords and other creatures which seldom attacked, frightened away by the barrier of magic that surrounded the lakeside villages. This day the mages would come to strengthen the barriers and the warning that pinched my mind told me I should have run. Was it too late?

The sharp knock at the door made my head jerk up. My heart thumped wildly as I dropped the stone and glanced at the window. Soon the flaming streaks of dawn would fill the shop with light. Swallowing hard, I wiped my hands on a cloth and made my way to the door. It was only an early customer in haste for a remedy from the apothecary. No one had discovered who I was, no one had come for me. Repeating the words like a mantra in my mind, I leaned against the door and called softly, so not to wake Donella, the owner of the apothecary. "What do you need?"

The knock came again, rough and impatient. The person on the other side must urgently need a remedy. Someone could be sick, or giving birth. Donella said she denied no one, but I only mixed potions and tinctures while she worked the counter. Even though concern twisted through me, I lifted the bar and opened the door.

Immediately the person on the other side pushed inside, filling the air with the musk of vanilla mixed with winter berries, pine and leather. I breathed in, calmed for a moment, then stumbled back, frowning at the lumbering man who closed the door behind him.

Not only was he a head taller than me, but broad shouldered. Thick white and gray furs concealed his upper body, making him appear even larger. Leather boots protected his feet all the way up to mid-calf. A hood obscured his face, but I glimpsed blond hair and shad-owed eyes. Berating myself for gawking, I stepped back, careful of the jars and vials behind me.

The shop was small, only a square room with a work table to one side, and wood shelves holding a mixture of recipe books, jars of dried herbs, powders and other ingredients, and vials of ready-made potions. It was my hiding place, for those who came for remedies did not indulge in gossip. They came with anxious, wide eyes, whispering their needs and slipped away. The apothecary kept the secrets of its customers. Silence was the key, and no one else questioned why I'd suddenly appeared three years ago or why I worked as an assistant to Donella.

Even though it was best to keep moving, I was comfortable now with the ebb and flow of the village. It sloped down to the shores of a lake which rushed away, who knew where, perhaps to the other side of the world. All I knew were the shores of the wild country which butted up against the forsaken mountains where the ice lords dwelled, barbaric and savage. The mages protected us from their murderous intentions. Without their magic, the ice lords would swoop down, kill the menfolk, and steal the women away for their own. It was a fate none dared speculate on. They ate raw meat and slept in blood. There was nothing but cold and monsters up there, far away from civilization. But down here I could enjoy the calming sound of the lake, the laughter of babies and the villagers going about their days hunting, farming and fishing.

I'd stayed because no one looked twice at me, or asked questions. Besides, it was easy to find the ingredients that kept the monster inside me from escaping, as it once had. The mages would not come for me though, not today, I vowed.

Returning to the worktable, I put it between myself and the man. It wasn't unusual for a man to visit the apothecary, yet he did not look familiar. After three years, I assumed I'd seen most of the villagers during the festivals that took place. Usually I stayed on the outskirts, a silent watcher who blended in without drawing attention to myself.

"What do you need?" I asked. Without looking up, I sensed the weight of his gaze on me and knew what he'd see.

I wore a plain woolen dress, light blue, the color of ice when reflected by the sun. I'd tied my black hair at the nape of my neck so it wouldn't interfere with my work. With my sleeves pushed up to my elbows, my arms were on display. I had dark skin, long limbs, a narrow oval face and bright brown eyes. Sometimes when I looked in the mirror, a sliver of blue stared back, causing a constricting fear to rise. No, I wouldn't think of it, I had control over my abilities as long as I stayed here, in hiding, in the apothecary.

"I need a liquid, something to make someone sleep well and long, something that works quickly." His low voice rumbled through the room, making the air shift, twist and scatter away from him, afraid of his power. There was something else uncanny about him that made the hairs on my arm stand up straight.

"You're wanting moon dust," I told him. Turning from the counter, I moved to the bottles, blowing on the shelf to chase away the dust. I pulled out a vial the size of my forefinger. Setting it on the table, I moved a safe distance back from the stranger. "It's made with a base of valerian root and passionflower to mask the sour taste. I recommend a few drops in a cup of tea before sleep to relax the body."

The man shifted. "How long does it last?"

"Eight to ten hours," I shrugged. "It's hard to know exactly."

"How quickly does it work? I need something that works fast."

I paused. While we did have stronger and faster-acting herbs, a slight misgiving twisted in my belly. The apothecary lived by a simple code of not harming others, but surely he wasn't planning to hurt someone.

"If you would," he stepped closer. "I'm in a bit of a hurry."

When he shook his head, his hood fell back. My mouth opened and closed as I stared up into the crystal blue eyes of an ice lord. A mane of thick blond hair was braided back from his forehead and fell to his shoulders. The shadow of a beard crossed his jawline, but the curves of his pointed ears gave him away for who he was... One of the fae.

Deep-set eyes framed by light eyelashes stared back at me, then flashed. His brow creased at my hesitation. I sensed the threat, the intent to frighten me into submission, but I drew myself upright. Not that I was brave, only that I couldn't be cowed by a fearsome ice lord when what was within me was more terrifying. His eyes fell to my bare neck and then away to the table. His next words were unexpected. "You need help?"

"No." My words came out faster, harder than intended. "I know what you need."

"Do you?" he arched an eyebrow almost playfully.

Heat warmed my cheeks as I set the next bottle on the table. "This is a tincture, but be careful. A few drops will

5

make one feel faint and dizzy, so make sure the draught is administered while lying down."

Licking his lips, he picked it up with a trembling hand. His furs fell away, revealing the markings on his hand and arms. Runes of sun, stars and a great winged beast, a dragon, drawn in a bold black ink. He froze, fingers on the neck of the bottle as his crystal blue eyes rose to my face.

Now I had the upper hand. "Take it," I waved the bottle away. "I know who you are and I will keep your secret, but I warn you. Ice lords are frowned upon here in Lansing Falls, especially today. You should leave before the mages arrive for the tithe. If they know you've trespassed, they'll hunt you down and kill you."

Tucking the vial away, he produced a coin. "Will this be enough?"

A golden coin with the head of a wolf, currency perhaps in the mountains, but it would do no good here. I stepped back. "Keep it."

White teeth flashed as he frowned. "I do not accept charity."

"None is given," I rebutted. "That coin is no good here. I cannot use it to barter and trade without suspicion. Take it. One day, perhaps, you'll be able to do a good deed in return."

With a grunt, he pulled his hood over his head, hiding his pointed ears. His long legs carried him across the small room in two steps and he pulled open the door. At the very last moment, he turned and touched two fingers to his heart. "My thanks are with you."

Surprising words for a fearsome ice lord. Dangerous

and yet I wasn't frightened. Instead, warmth radiated in my belly, the satisfaction of another happy customer as the door shut firmly behind him. I thought about bolting it again, but the sun was almost fully awake now and Donella would stir. Besides, I hadn't finished my own potion.

Returning to the stone I continued to grind the herbs into a fine powder then poured it into the liquid over the fire. I stirred it slowly, letting everything blend together. When it cooled, I'd bottle it up, another week's supply of the medicine that helped me keep my sanity. Even now I felt the darkness clawing inside me, begging to escape. But I wouldn't let it. Not again.

CHAPTER 2

"Solvay." A voice laced with disapproval pulled me away from my work. "You aren't going like that, are you?"

"Donella." I tightened the lid on the last vial and set it on the shelf. "I'm almost ready, let me grab my cloak."

Donella wasn't as young as she used to be, nor was she elderly. Despite her tiny size and the stoop of her shoulders, her elfin face was smooth and eyes kind. When I'd first met her, I thought she knew more than she said with her penetrating gaze that looked beyond. I wondered if she had the gift of sight, to see the future, yet aside from making healing remedies there was no magic, only a deep knowledge and the regret she had no children to pass it to. She and her husband had run the apothecary until he passed away. Now it was hers, and I thought she was lonesome sometimes, working in the shop by herself. Her dark hair was braided around the crown of her head, and she also wore a simple gown, although she faulted me for it because I wasn't past the marrying age.

"They aren't all bad," Donella called as I pulled on my wool cloak.

"The mages?" I frowned and turned my back to her. Lifting the bottle from my pocket, I swallowed the contents. It burned going down, and the aftertaste made me want to gag. My eyes filled with tears but I blinked them back, pocketed the empty bottle and turned to face Donella.

"Some have found themselves happy with the match. You might too."

Shaking my head, I moved to the door. "No, I don't want a match, and I certainly don't want to catch the eye of a mage. I go because I must, they'll know if we don't, but I will stand in the back and avoid their gaze, like I do every year."

"Posh Solvay." Donella took my offered arm and squeezed it. "You can't live and work in the apothecary forever, you can't end up like me. You're young and smart, surely you want more than this?"

By 'this' she meant the life she led. A lump grew in my throat, choking out my words. Of course I wanted to be normal and live without fear of myself. I wanted a lot of things, but none of them were possible. I was doing the best I could under the circumstances.

We stepped outside to the cool breeze of spring. The air was still nippy, but the promise of warmth hung like a faint memory. I gathered my cloak tighter around my shoulders and pulled up the hood, grateful for warm gloves and boots. The village sloped downhill, built in a series of levels and narrow roads and buildings that all curved down to the harbor. The cobblestone streets rang under booted feet, but the nervousness of the people soured the air. I felt it too, that silent trepidation that something bad would happen.

We rounded a bend and came to the stairs that led down to the square by the lake. Five ships floated on the lake, carved in the shape of a giant kittiwake, complete with wings that stretched out, the sails that kept them going as they flew over the waters. Unlike the villages, the mages did not sail with oars and sails; they used their magic to propel themselves over the choppy waters, going where they pleased. I knew without doubt it was their magic that forced the villagers to bow and give them anything and everything they wanted without complaint, for who dared disobey such power?

A hush fell over the gathering as we descended the stairs. Silver flags blew in the breeze and the chill of winter stole across the waters like searching fingers, filtering through the warmth of my cloak, prying, seeking. I stepped behind a tall man and paused, unwilling to expose myself further to the cold and the seeking eyes of the mages. They emerged from the ships, a party of bright colors like a peacock, trying to woo the women with a false beauty that soon evaporated under the coolness of their hearts.

I always wondered what happened to them, the women who were chosen as brides for the mages. Were they warm and happy, did they eat fine foods and learn magic, or were they kept in harems? It all happened so quickly. The mages came, chose, then swept the women away in broad ships off to the palace.

We could see it from the shore, a castle perched on a flat mountaintop, like an all-seeing eye keeping watch. Once the ice melted, the mages descended, although some lived in the village year-round to ensure people kept their laws and the magical barriers did not falter.

No one spoke the truth out loud, but we knew the mages came to our village because of rumors of magic. Magic flourished close to the mountains, and with each child that was born, the mages would come and hope to raise them as one of their own. The second tithe happened in the fall, when the mages came to test the children, those ages five to ten to see if they had magic in their blood and abilities that could be groomed for the army of mages.

They were taken away on those ships too; I didn't know if they returned, for no one spoke about it, but I'd heard the mothers weeping, crying in the dark of night when they thought the mages were gone and would not hear them mourning for a life that was lost. To them, at least. I wondered if the children suffered under the tutelage of mages, or grew strong, stern and powerful, forgetting their birth, forgetting where they came from.

Perhaps it was better to become a bride, to be taken by the mages and always with one's children. I put my head down, suppressing my thoughts as a trumpet blew, announcing the beginning. I clasped my fingers together as a voice soared over the waters, much like the kittiwake, announcing the mages. It was the last phrase that made my head jerk up and my heart hammer.

"Announcing his imperial majesty, King Adler of Lansing Falls. We have gathered today for the annual tithe, but this year is different. The seer has granted a vision to the king of his bride to be, a woman from this village who shall strengthen the line of mages."

I could not breathe. My throat constricted. The old, familiar ache in my chest began, the clawing of a beast fighting to get out. Despite the cold, a wave of heat passed over me. Magic. The mage spoke of magical children and power. Why hadn't I listened to my heart and fled before this day?

A hand on the small of my back brought me back to the moment. "It's time," Donella encouraged. "Go ahead to the center, it will be okay."

I'd missed the call, the invitation for all unmarried women to step forward. It wasn't truly an invitation, but an order. Again, that uncanny flare of magic twisted through the air, almost yanking at my skirts, as though it knew who I was, young, unwed. I had to step forward.

The crowd jostled, letting women through to stand in front of the speaker, in front of those ships. A hint of gold filled my vision as King Adler came into view. Someone took my arm and pulled me forward, murmuring, "It will be over soon."

It was a woman who had visited the shop a few days ago. She'd asked for a potion to calm the pains in her belly, the painful cramps that forced her to stay in bed. Now was not the time to ask her how she felt.

Silently, I counted as the group gathered. Thirty unwed women. Surely there had been more the year before. Had so many married after the tithe? Spring was the time for matchmaking. Celebrations and ceremonies took place as the first May flowers bloomed and the threat of one last snow faded for good.

Holding the skirt of my dress with my fingers, I held still, as though pretending to be a statue would save me from being chosen. The mages used magic to choose their brides, determining who would bless their bloodline. They also kept a registry of the villagers. I'd never registered with the mages, hadn't seen the need, and hoped it might prevent me from being chosen.

The mage read a list of names from a scroll, and as each name was spoken, a woman stepped forward. Five names were called. Five brides for the mages. The mage closed the scroll, eyes narrowed, and stared at the assembly. I kept my head bowed, refusing to look. To make eye contact could be disastrous.

The crowd gasped, the clip of a boot echoed and then a shadow stood in front of me, blocking me from the wind. A finger touched my chin, lifting it up to focus on the eyes of the mage king. "You," he said, smiling, "You will be the bride of the king."

CHAPTER 3

J stared into golden eyes and the clawing within grew stronger. He wasn't much taller than me and yet his presence swelled, filling the air with his aura. The luster of his eyes seemed unnatural against his dark beard and wavy black hair, yet the gold band in his hair matched his eyes, and I could not miss the blue and silver ring on his finger. He was handsome, the angles and slopes of his face so magnificent it was difficult to look away.

Swallowing down my dismay, I took a deep breath. My fears could not get the best of me to the detriment of all. As I calmed myself, breathing out of my parted lips, the mage king dropped his hand, although his fingers grazed my arm, sending a cold shiver up my spine. "What is your name?"

His voice was warm, slow like honey. As soon as the vibrance of his words drifted to my ears, I knew it was magic. Why would he use magic on his bride to be?

"Solvay," I replied.

"Solvay." He smiled, although his eyes remained cold. "You will be my bride."

It wasn't a question but a statement to inform me of my fate. My heart sank to my toes. King of the mages. He did not appear much older than me, which made me wonder why he was king, and what had made him in such a hurry for a bride. Perhaps the line of mages was dying out, and they needed more children and more magic. I tightened my fingers into fists beneath my cloak, sinking into a bow as he remained merely a breath away.

"I'm honored." The words came out mechanically because it was what I must say. I'd never seen anyone reject a mage and only assumed what might happen to a woman should she refuse.

"Come." He held out his hand. "We will go to my kingdom."

So soon? I dared not let my anxiety show, but I could not go with him. What if he found out the truth about me? Who I was? What I kept locked inside? What might happen if I lost control and turned into my "other" self, where the darkness was relentless?

Thoughts flashed through my mind as he took my hand and raised it high. People clapped and congratulated me while the other mages stepped forward with their brides. Six in all. We'd enter those ships and be escorted across the lake to the palace. Despite what I believed about the mages, I couldn't go. Women and children lived up there, and I would end them all.

Moving to the king's side, I squeezed his hand, leaned closer and lowered my voice. Silky, sultry words came out. "Your Majesty, I am honored you chose me, but I ask

15

for this request before we depart. I have a few valuable items at home I wish to bring with me, small things that will fit in a bag, trinkets I hold valuable. Will you but give me a few moments to collect those before we leave?"

When his gaze met mine, that clawing sensation grew stronger. He examined me as though he could read my mind, then nodded. "My men shall go with you. We leave within the hour."

That's always how it was. The arrival. The selection. The departure. All done quickly, as though they could not bear to be on the land a moment longer than necessary and away from their gilded kingdom. A kingdom which would be my prison, my demise.

I should have felt some semblance of relief that he'd answered my request, and sending his men with me was logical. They wouldn't want me out of their sight, as if I could run away. I barely heard Donella wish me well as two mages followed me up the stairs, back to the apothecary.

The streets were quiet, the tension thick as the people waited for the mages to leave, so they could celebrate or grieve. That was the hardest part about the tithe. Those who were left behind had to deal with what had happened, with whom they might never see again. Families were divided, lovers parted, but most put on a good face and gathered to comfort those left behind, especially those who grieved. The tithe for brides was never as horrible as the tithe for children.

As the apothecary appeared, I stepped inside, mouth dry and eyed the shelves. "I'll be just a moment," I told the mages who guarded the door. Summoning my courage, I reached for the potion I'd made that morning, enough to last me for a week if not more.

Ducking into the back hall, I entered my small room. Quickly, I snatched up the few things I'd need. Rolling the bottle in a scarf so it would not break, I slipped it into a bag along with the other items that were already packed. Long ago, I'd learned it was smart to be prepared to flee at any moment, and the bag was ready with the essentials I'd need until I found another quiet village, a place to start over. My fingers trembled and the demon inside clawed as I tip-toed out of the room.

Unfortunately, the shop did not have a back door, but it had a window which led out into the dark alley between buildings where chamber pots and other rubbish were dumped. The air was thick and sour until the rains washed away the filth.

Peeking back to ensure the mages did not suspect me, I opened the window. It stuck at first, then gave way with a sharp whine of protest. My pulse sped up as I tossed the bag into the street, then pushed my head out. Foul air made me wrinkle my nose, but my desperation was greater. Wiggling my head and shoulders, I used my feet to push myself upward and pull myself out. At the last moment, I lost my balance and tumbled into the street. A bolt of pain shot up my shoulder, but there was no time. Gasping, I snatched up my bag, looped it over my shoulders and ran.

The alley led uphill, further into the twisting roads of the village. But I knew, ultimately, where it would go. A soft curse rang out behind me, and then footsteps. Already? Surely the mages wouldn't fit through the window. Had they seen me, or had their magic alerted them to my flight? I had no idea how their magic worked. Still, I was light and fast.

I turned a corner and ducked down another ally. I'd walked this route before, tracked it up through the village and out the outer gates. They were old and used to keep the wild creatures from coming through. The mages used magic to keep them shut and after each tithe walked through the city, sealing it with their wards of protection. The gates were at their weakest on the day of the tithe, and I'd be able to slip through. Unless, somehow, the mages used their magic to restrain me.

If they caught me... No. I wouldn't speculate but focus on the primary goal. Keeping my freedom.

The gates rose before me, mighty and strong. Solid oak made up their walls, built in a hurry, yet time had been taken to build a gatehouse, a smaller entrance for those to come and go. As I approached, the small door stood wide open, showing me thick pine trees, the way into the wood and up farther into the mountains where the ice lords dwelt.

No one came this way, so why was the gate open?

The footsteps behind me quickened, and I hastened my speed, torn between pulling the door shut behind me or leaving it open. In the end, my need for speed won out and I burst through the gate into the woods.

The ground inclined sharply, throwing me off balance. My side ached and my lungs burned. It was warmer under the trees, surprising, for I'd always considered the village warm. I had to lose my pursuer, but when I darted into the forest, brambles crunched underfoot. I was making too much noise to hide. Soon the mages would catch up and I'd be on the ship with the golden eyes of the mage king staring at me. As if he knew...

That thought urged me forward just as my cloak caught on a branch. I spun, grasping with one hand to tug it free when something, no someone, grabbed me from behind. An arm went around my waist, yanking me back against a hard, warm body.

I kicked out, fighting as hard as I could. I needed a branch, a stick, something to knock him down, and then a cloth pressed against my nose. A familiar smell came over me as I breathed in and blackness took me.

CHAPTER 4

J expected to wake on the ship of the mage king while he glared at me out of glittering eyes and announced my punishment for running. What would it be? A night in the dungeon? A whipping? Some other horrible lesson to make me regret my actions? Or maybe this time only a stern word. But I didn't feel the rocking of waves.

Opening my eyes, I stared into the gaze of... Not the mage king but a strange, shaggy beast. It had long white hair, horns that curled back, claws instead of hooves. Doe-like round eyes stared back at me before the beast shook its head and lay back down.

So I was already in the dungeons. Watched over by... What was that creature? My bag was still slung over my shoulder, the floor was made of stones but an odd blue aura surrounded me. The sound of chimes or the tinkling of silver bells rang in my ears. I fought back the clawing inside. First, I'd assess my situation and make a level-headed decision. Perhaps there was a way out of this after all. All I needed to do was wait for another audience with the king. Surely he'd be a reasonable man.

I hadn't been bound, which was a relief, but doubts whispered like the breath of wind as I searched for something to use as a weapon. There was a scarf and maybe some rope in my bag. Opening it, I noted everything was as I'd placed it. Odd they hadn't taken it, or at least rifled through it. I stood and the ground beneath me shifted, the color changing from a bluish tint to gold. I stumbled back. Was it magic?

A rustle followed by a thonk made me whirl around, pressing myself against the curved wall of the dungeon. No fear, I would show no fear. Straightening my shoulders, I lifted my chin. But it was not the mage king.

A man fed another log to a nearby fire, the wood thumping against itself. Gathering my surroundings, I lay on a rock ledge only a short distance from the man and the shadows of what might be trees. I was in a cave.

My brow furrowed in confusion. I was sure the mages had caught me. Was this an illusion meant to trick me? I crept toward the fire as the man stood. My vision went dizzy then cleared as all my expectations evaporated like ice melting in the fierce sun. I pressed a hand to my heart, unsure whether to be deeply relieved or erratically angry. No, the man wasn't the mage king at all. The daylight pouring in the cave entrance clearly allowed me to see it was the ice lord who'd visited the apothecary this morning.

It all came rushing back, the chase, the hand grabbing me and the cloth pressed against my face. I'd been undone by my own potion. No wonder the scent was so familiar. "You!" I pointed a finger, anger surging out at my last word.

Without the slightest rush, he dusted his fingers, stood straight and folded his arms across his chest. He'd discarded his furs, lying them around the fire like rugs, as though he were some royalty who needed furs to walk upon. "You're awake," he stated nonchalantly. "The effects wore off quickly."

My hands shook as rage rose in me and I clenched them by my side. "You... You... Why am I here? What did you do?"

Despite my need to be calm, my voice rose almost to a scream.

The strange white fur-beast rose with a grunt and trotted up beside me.

"Down Wilbur." The ice lord lifted a hand, palm down.

The fur-beast, Wilbur, sat on his hindquarters.

I eyed the entrance to the cave. The dark golden hue of the sky told me it was near sunset, six hours since the tithe. An icy trickle of fear went down my spine. "The mage king will come for me."

"That I don't doubt," the obnoxious ice lord agreed, raising his eyebrows in amusement. "You did not look as though you wanted to be chosen by the king. I saw you climb out the window and run away, which made my task much easier. Thank you for that."

"What task?" I growled through gritted teeth.

He scratched his head. "Look, er... I didn't know it was going to be you. I went to the village to do something wicked, steal the mage king's bride. Don't worry, I'll return you to him unharmed. I just need leverage."

"Worry?" I tried to laugh, but it came out strangled. "You kidnapped me and you tell me not to worry, like you have some brilliant plan. If the mages find you, they'll kill you and ask questions later."

"Not if I have you," he disagreed.

A muscle in my cheek jumped and the darkness in the pit of my being surged, begging to be let out. "You had no right to take me. I gave you a potion in good faith, believing you would use it as a remedy, not to steal a woman! You're just as bad as them."

His eyes flashed, and the mirth left his face, replaced with something dangerous. I stepped back, forgetting about Wilbur and almost tripped over him. My arms flailed as I caught my balance.

"Listen, woman." His tone was hard, clipped. "Like I said before, no harm will come to you. Soon enough you'll return to the mage king, just give me time. Now, do I need to tie you up or will you come sit by the fire and eat?"

He spoke to me as though I were a child, but I knew exactly who I was. His prisoner. I sized him up again. He was broad and tall with rippling muscles. My eyes went to the axe by his side, the knives in his belt. He was well armed, and I'd already forgotten about Wilbur, who could take me down in a moment if I fled. I was truly stuck, trapped with a dangerous ice lord, subjected to his whim, whatever that might be. There was nothing left to do but stay level-headed. Soon an opportunity would present itself. He'd let down his guard, and I'd flee.

Besides, I was cold, my throat sore, and my head ached from inhaling such a strong dosage of the potion. Folding my hands across my chest, I glared at him. "I'd like some water, but know this, ice lord, just because I sit and eat a meal with you tonight does not make us friends."

"I would hardly expect that," he retorted.

Still, he went to some bags I hadn't noticed before and pulled out a water skin. Standing, he tossed it toward me.

I paused before taking a drink. What if he'd added more of the potion to the water? I sniffed, then took a sip. When nothing happened, I took another, suddenly feeling refreshed. Keeping my eye on the man, I put the fire between us and sat down on the furs. They were softer than I expected and the fire was warm, comforting.

We sat in silence. Him feeding the fire and turning whatever he was cooking over a spit and me, drinking water and trying not to glower at him. I had to admit, in a way he'd saved me from the mages, but I couldn't help that dark knowing inside. He meant to return me to them, which meant I was his hostage. What did he need so badly that he was willing to capture me and then trade me back to the mages in exchange?

CHAPTER 5

*T*ension stretched between us, thick and unsavory. I stared into the flames, leaping and dancing as they licked up the wood. With each flicker, my anger subsided from the roar of a wave to a trickle. This was only a momentary setback, but I needed more information before I ran away. Besides traveling with this woody ice lord could have its benefits. Although as I looked across the fire at him, my optimistic outlook faded. He looked like the kind of man who always got what he wanted, and those who stood in his way perished.

Turning my gaze away from the glint of his axe, I opened my mouth. "Where—"

At the same time, he glanced at me. "What—"

We both broke off. I pressed my lips together to keep the words from spilling out. After an awkward silence, he went on. "What is your name?"

"Solvay, and yours?" I stared at the fire, unwilling to meet those piercing blue eyes.

"Ayden." He picked up a small piece of wood and attacked it with his knife.

"Ayden," I repeated, straightening my shoulders. "I hope we can come to an agreement. You are currently holding me against my will intending to return me to the mage king who holds no ownership over me. You must let me go."

"Must." He grunted. His knife peeled away the outer layers, showing the smooth, pale insides of the wood. "It's not unusual for women to desire to escape an arranged marriage."

I bristled. "How would you know what women want?"

Pausing, he looked across the fire at me and something flickered in his eyes. "My wife ran, at first."

Wife. Ah. So he was married. I didn't know why, but the slightest bit of disquiet awoke in me. It bothered me, the fact that a married man clearly had no respect for women and set off to kidnap whoever the mage king choose to be his bride. "Then you have learned very little about women," I retorted. "Your wife was right to run off since you have no respect for ladies. Ah, I forget, you're an ice lord. One of the fae. It is your nature."

He froze and his eyes clouded like a storm moving across the sky. There was darkness there and something else, sorrow? Regret? I'd hurled my words at him because I had nothing else, but my frustration manifested somehow and I'd wounded him. Just as quickly, he returned to whittling the wood. "Aye, you have a sharp tongue. It is true. I haven't known many women, and my wife died before I got the chance. Remarrying does not seem urgent since my brother carries the family line and I have bigger concerns."

His wife was dead? I wondered how that had happened. Perhaps he'd gotten angry and strangled her. I glanced at his big hands and long fingers. There was enough strength in them to do dastardly things. With a snort, I latched on to his last words. "Bigger concerns? Like kidnapping me."

Dropping his woodwork, he glared across the fire. "Are you always like this with your quick tongue and biting words? This will make a sore and long journey."

"How else would it be?" I returned. "Remember, you kidnapped me, and you expect me to be pleasant company?"

We glowered across the fire at each other. I all but felt the heat of his anger, burning brighter and hotter. If not for his wretched beast, I'd dash out of the cave. Although I was light and quick, he'd caught me once and he might catch me again. I needed a different plan.

At last, his shoulders relaxed, he reached for his waist and pulled something out of a bag. The coin. The gold coin I'd turned down in the shop. He flicked it over to me and I caught it with both hands. Before I could open my mouth to protest, he spoke.

"Lady Solvay, you were kind to me in the shop and I remember your words. You asked me to do a good deed in exchange. I cannot let you walk free, not yet, but I would be willing to strike a bargain with you."

I squeezed the coin in my palm. It was warm from his pocket. A bargain. "I'm not sure what kind of bargain I would trust, especially from an ice lord."

He pressed a hand to his heart. "On my honor, I will not allow any harm to come to you from now until you return to the mage king."

Honor? An ice lord? The irony of his words made me want to laugh, but the solemn look on his face pricked my conscience. Now was the time for honesty. "Your words mean nothing to me when you intend to return me to the mage king at the end of whatever this is. I didn't run because I was afraid, I ran because I can't go there, I can't go to the dark halls of the mages. It will be the utter ruin of all. I ran to save the village, to save the people, and returning me will only lead to destruction. I want to go far, far away from here and if you can take me away or point me to the right road, I will gladly go."

The color drained from his face. "You don't understand." His voice was rough. "I can't just let you go. I need to make a deal with the mages, one that will benefit my people, that will allow us to come down from the mountains to trade, to farm. We can't stay up in the mountains, starving. I would see an end to the oppression of my people and it begins with you. I need something the mages desperately want. And if I can offer him you in exchange... to give my people hope, then I must."

I bit my bottom lip. An ice lord with a heart? Why couldn't he be a ruthless, evil man on a horrible quest? Why did he want to do something honorable? Suddenly I wondered if everything I knew about the ice lords was a lie. A falsehood told by the mages to keep the villagers frightened, to make them lock the gates and shut their doors, to allow for the tithe and the magical wards of protection. Were we the ones who place blind faith in the mages, hoping they would save us when they were the reason for oppression?

Blinking back tears of frustration, I stared at the coin, flipping it over in my fingers, as if the movement would help me make up my mind. Doom swirled, perhaps what I'd felt that morning in the shop. This was the warning I'd sensed.

"If you pursue this, you're going to start a war."

He crossed his arms over his chest and stared out at the darkening sky. "Then so be it."

CHAPTER 6

I slept badly that night, tossing and turning on the furs, hating that they smelled like him. Leather and winter berries with hints of vanilla. He'd kidnapped me, but I didn't know whether it was better to be with him or the mages. Questions raced through my mind. What had happened to Donella after my disappearance? Was Ayden right? Would the mage king come after me?

The mages were a proud people. They would not take the insult of a runaway bride lightly. Especially since they believed the fates guided them, showing them visions of whom to pick to continue the line of mages. Pressing a hand to my flat belly, a wave of sorrow made my throat tight. Any child I bore would have magic, and they'd be cursed, like me. A monster resting inside, waiting to erupt.

My gaze flickered to Ayden's sleeping form, unaware of what I was, and the damage I could do if I lost my restraint and went wild. He was so sure the mages would hunt us down, which made me wonder why we were sleeping in a cave if they were coming. Why did Ayden think he could stand against the magic of mages? There had to be something else he wasn't telling me, for he appeared calm, calculated without fear. Perhaps it was just desperation. If his plan went wrong, many would suffer.

My musing drowned out the need for sleep, besides the potion he'd drugged me with had worn off, leaving me wide awake. Every time I opened my eyes, Wilbur lifted his head and glared right back at me. When I sat up, a low growl came out of his throat. No wonder I wasn't tied up, there was no escape, not unless I wanted to run only to be mauled down by Wilbur. Fine. I lay back down and waited while the lights in the cave shifted from blue to silver and then black.

It was still dark when Ayden rose, gathering the furs and bundling them into a pack he secured on his back. Wordlessly I joined him and we stepped out into the dawn, Wilbur at our heels. I took a sharp breath and my eyes were pulled in four directions. Snow covered the ground and trees swallowed us so it was impossible to tell which way was forward and which way was back.

The scent of pine filled the air, and a cool wind made my exposed skin tingle. I peered back toward the cave, hidden unless one knew where to look. Ayden strode ahead, the pack on his back, moving skillfully, silently, as though he were a creature of the wood.

"Where are we?" I asked, lifting my skirts in one hand as I followed in his footsteps.

"In the hills above Lansing Falls," he called over his shoulder.

A tree shook its branches, sending a cascade of snow raining down on my head. I brushed it off, glaring at it. "Where are we going?"

"To my home in the mountains." He paused, as though he intended to say more, then continued walking, ending the brief conversation.

Mountains. I'd be far away from the mages, but would it be far enough? Regardless of what happened, I needed to be vigilant. As soon as Ayden let down his guard, I'd run. To save myself, save everyone. If only he knew the darkness he was leading to his doorstep.

I studied the forest for help, but it was silent aside from the wind and the occasional fall of snow. "How long will it take to get there?"

"Less than a fortnight if we make good time," he called.

I tucked that knowledge away. Plenty of time for me to figure out my surroundings and make a plan to escape. As if reading my thoughts, Wilbur nosed against me, reminding me to keep moving.

The patches of snow were thin as we continued, following an invisible path I assumed Ayden knew from memory.

I followed in his footsteps, my irritation growing as the day passed. Ayden was quiet too, heedless of the cold and my growing anger. Unease crept around me as the sun set, and an opportunity to flee hadn't presented itself.

We rested that night, hidden by the boughs of trees, the thick branches protecting us from the wind. I spent it silent and stewing, glaring at Ayden who didn't seem to notice my anger.

In the morning we trudged on, and by mid-morning, we reached a ridge. When I looked back, tiny clouds of snow rose, hiding our footprints like some kind of sorcery. I glared at the snow through narrowed eyes and it flattened back down, as though it thought better of its imprudence to hide. Trees swallowed us on all sides, but a rustling in the woods reminded me that Ayden, Wilbur and I weren't the only ones in the wood.

The rustling continued until a buck stepped out of the trees, liquid brown eyes studying us beneath the antlers on his head. Brown fur had hints of white on it and my lips parted, enchanted by his fearless beauty.

Something flashed out of the corner of my eye. An arrow sank into the shoulder of the beast. It brayed and ran, dashing back into a grove. Wilbur dashed after it and I whirled, unreasonable anger rising within to glare at Ayden. He'd dropped his hands to his side and watched.

"Why?" I demanded. "It was just watching us. Why did you shoot it?"

His expression hardened as he tied the bow on his back. "Wilbur has to eat, same as we do. A fresh kill will last much longer than the dried meat I carry."

I bristled, well aware my anger was misplaced. Wouldn't I have done the same if I were traveling through the wood? A buck had many uses, not only for food, but its skin would serve as leather for a cloak or boots.

Ayden trudged on without waiting for a response and I hurried to catch up. "We aren't waiting for Wilbur?"

"He'll rejoin us later, after he's had his fill." He eyed

me, eyebrows raised and my cheeks warmed under his scrutiny. "Besides, you don't want to watch him eat. It is unsavory."

I turned away from his piercing eyes, hoping my question would deflect his attention. "What kind of creature is Wilbur? I've never seen a beast like him."

As I'd hoped, Ayden shifted his gaze, following Wilbur's footprints in the snow. His tone gentled. "There are many wonders up here in the mountains, unnamed creatures both beautiful and terrifying. I admit, I don't know exactly what Wilbur is. I found him during a hunt. His mother lay dead, likely fighting off some beast that had eaten his brothers and sisters. At first, I thought he was dead too until he whimpered. He was still alive, but just barely. I've had him ever since. He's most similar to a wolf. I believe he prefers to hunt in a pack which is why I shot the buck. The wounded animal will still fight, but Wilbur can experience the thrill of the hunt. He doesn't mind scraps from the table but he's a wild young one. He needs a fresh kill to sate him."

Those words stuck with me: the thrill of a hunt and kill.

As if answering, the darkness inside me ballooned, responding to those words because it, too, needed the thrill of utter destruction before it grew sated, calmed. Unlike Wilbur, hunting and killing a buck would not be enough. I needed more to calm my bloodlust, my need for destruction. With trembling fingers, I opened my bag and fumbled around inside for a potion.

"What's wrong?" His hand came under my arm, offering me his strength.

Suddenly I felt weak, my strength sucked away. "I just need to sit down for a moment. My medicine," I gasped.

Gently, he guided me down until I leaned against a tree.

"Sit with me," I begged, pressing a hand to my heart.

His eyes widened at my labored breathing, concern making his lips go tight. "Do you need water?"

Moving closer, he opened his pack, searching for the waterskin.

I took a resolute breath, lifted my bag, and smashed it into his skull.

Set off balance, Ayden fell forward. I heard the jarring crack of his head whack into the tree trunk, but I didn't wait. Leaping to my feet, bag in hand, I fled as if the mages were behind me.

CHAPTER 7

The shallow dusting of snow churned beneath my feet as I continued toward the ridge, then zigzagged into the trees, cursing. I didn't know much about the terrain. Ayden had the edge on me, but Wilbur was hunting and this was my one chance to escape.

As I ran, my mind returned to a memory, buried deep and yet resurfacing. Blood on my hands, bare feet running across the frozen ground, sending a spray of white mist into the air behind me. Then, I hadn't fled because I was being hunted; I was trying to outrun myself, my urges, and what had the potential to drive me mad.

My vision blurred as I tried to forget the memory. It had been so long ago. I'd survived and moved past that moment. I was no longer a skinny fifteen-year-old with blood on my hands, although the monster still lurked inside, waiting to break free.

Once my vision cleared, I spied a pile of gray stones near an outcropping of pine trees, tall enough for me to hide behind. Just in time, too, for a curse rang out behind me. Ayden was coming.

I started down the ridge. The incline wasn't steep, but I slipped. Soft snow suddenly hardened into ice. Impossible, yet I lost my footing and fell heavily on my back. Pain radiated up my tailbone and breath whooshed out of me. A moment later, Ayden was on top of me, his powerful hands pressed against my shoulders, pinning me down while he straddled me. Blood poured down the side of his head where I'd bashed it into the tree.

My chest squeezed, sending me back into the memory. I kicked, but my legs were trapped beneath him. When I brought my hands up to claw at his face, he knocked them away.

"Let go of me!" I screamed.

A calloused hand clamped down on my mouth. He leaned so close I caught the wet shimmer in his blue eyes, but my eyes were riveted to a single drop of blood rolling down his cheek. Instead of wiping it away, his gaze darted to the left, towards my would-be stone hiding place.

When he spoke, his voice was barely above a whisper. "Don't. Move."

I couldn't move anyway, since his weight held me down, but the timber of his voice made me shiver with fear. I followed his gaze as a cracking sound split the air, like ice melting on the lake.

The rock stretched and then stood up, revealing arms, legs and a stony face.

My throat went dry, my limbs limp, and my lips parted. A shallow breath whistled out of my mouth as I stared. I'd heard legends of impossible monsters made of stone, but I hadn't believed them until now.

The rock wasn't a rock at all, but a golem. A creature made in the image of a man and then brought to life by dark magic. Sorcery. A creature made of the dreams of mages.

The golem turned, hollow sockets staring at us, and took a step.

The ground trembled as it moved, and Ayden's hand slid away from my mouth. His fingers dug into my shoulders as he yanked me to his chest, rolling us away from the golem. Just as suddenly he let go.

"Run!"

My desire to live overrode my fear. Scrambling to my feet, I continued my flight, this time back the way we'd come, running between the scattered trees. When I glanced over my shoulder, my heart lurched. Ayden was nowhere in sight. What was he doing?

Horror dawned on me. Ayden had just saved my life. If the snow hadn't turned to ice, and if he hadn't landed on top of me, I would have run straight into the golem and been crushed to death.

I spun to a stop. Moving behind a tree, I listened for his quick pants or boots thumping the ground, but I heard nothing. Biting the inside of my cheek, I considered what to do. No. Why was I waiting? This was my chance to escape while Ayden fought the golem. By the time he finished, I'd be long gone and his head injury would make it difficult to track me.

I gathered my skirts in my hands and took a step, but guilt brought me to another halt. I didn't care about the ice lord. He'd done me a great wrong by kidnapping me, and yet... I couldn't leave him to his death. Enough blood was already on my hands. Besides I was the one with the monster inside. I should be the one to fight the golem.

Except for one problem. I'd recently taken the potion to repress the monster. It wouldn't come out.

A roar brought me out of my conflicting thoughts, followed by a groan and then the thump as something large crashed to the ground. Forgetting about my safety, I leapt out of my hiding place and sprinted toward the sound.

It didn't take long to reach the ridge again, and I slowed to a stop, my heart fluttering wildly in my chest. Ayden stood at the bottom of the hill, hands raised, and the golem lay on its belly in front of him.

Gasping, I pressed a hand to my mouth. Golems were made of rock. It was impossible to defeat them.

"Ayden?" I called and made my way toward him.

With a jerk, he turned to face me, bringing his hands down. The light glinted on his fair head and shards of ice covered the ground surrounding him and the golem.

My brow furrowed. I did not see a weapon in his hands, only the glimmering patch of ice and the blood that stained his furs.

"Are you..." The words died in my throat. I paused just short of reaching out to touch him, because I wanted to hug him and sob my relief into his arms. I was relieved my captor hadn't died at the hands of the golem.

"It's dead," he breathed, taking a step away from it.

He swayed, and this time I couldn't stop myself from

taking his arm. "You need to sit down, eat something, recover your strength," I fussed.

"Not here." He waved his hand at the golem. "We need to press on a bit."

"Then lean on me." I tugged his arm over my shoulder and wrapped an arm around his waist. "Which way?"

He made a noise in his throat, somewhere between a laugh and grunt, as though amused by my actions. I gritted my teeth, keeping the retort inside, ignoring the scent of blood and leather and winter berries.

Together we walked until we were a fair distance from the fallen golem and under the trees again. I helped Ayden maneuver to the ground, and he leaned against a tree trunk, eyes closed, while I fumbled in my bag for a cloth. Using the waterskin, I cleaned his head, biting my lip at what I'd done to him.

Donella had treated a few head injuries, but there wasn't much she could do other than offer rest. Usually moon dust helped and for the first time, I began to worry. What would I do out here with an ice lord who was wounded? Wilbur was missing, and I had a notion there were more feral and deadly creatures in the mountains than I'd imagined.

Ayden kept his eyes closed as I wiped away the blood, revealing a deep gash in his head, but nothing that wouldn't heal. I did not have the tools to stich the skin back together, so I tied a clean cloth around his head to keep it from becoming infected.

When I finished, he opened his eyes, his lips curling up into a half-smile. Suddenly I was aware of how close I was to him as he reached up to touch my hand. When his fingers grazed my wrist, a spark the color of white lightning flashed between us.

Warmth flooded my cheeks, and I pulled back, breaking the slight contact. A blur of images danced before my mind, along with the urge to lean into his touch and breathe him in. What was I thinking? Thoughts of desire should be banished. He was a wild ice lord with no respect for women who probably drank blood when I wasn't looking.

Besides, my dark appetite for destruction meant I had to keep to myself, stay alone, move frequently, and never let the truth catch up with me. I couldn't get close to anyone, especially not the fae. Desire was forbidden, because if I let down my guard, the monster would surge forth and destroy everything and everyone I loved. Again.

"Thank you," he whispered, his voice thick.

Blinking, I met his gaze, unwilling to move, to break the spell, the softness that hung between us. Hard to believe earlier this morning I'd despised him.

"Don't thank me." I frowned at the bandage. "I'm the one who did this to you. As soon as Wilbur left, I saw my chance and... I wasn't aware of the dangers here."

A slow grin came to his face and those blue eyes turned mocking. "Wait... Did you just apologize, to me?"

I sighed as his fingers curled around my wrist, sending more shots of warmth through my veins. "Yes." I lifted my chin. "Enjoy this moment, it will be the last time it happens."

"Oh. I am enjoying this." His grin widened before

turning into a wince. He touched his head with his free hand.

"You should rest," I urged.

"And have you run away again? I think not."

"I'm not going to run."

He tilted his head, sizing me up. "You're a challenge, you know. I've never met a woman so intent on having her way."

"Probably because you never kidnapped a woman before," I retorted.

A flush replaced his cocky expression and guilt crept into his eyes. "No. I shouldn't have done it. I was desperate and... It was a foolish thing to do, the only way I could see to help my people."

I nodded, surprised he'd apologized. "No, it wasn't right." Pausing, I considered what would be best. I needed to get away from Lansing Falls, and I didn't know the mountain paths. Traveling with Ayden for a time was beneficial for my needs, except for the fact that he intended to give me back to them. I shuddered. I could not become the mage king's bride. "I don't understand why the mages haven't picked up our trail yet, if the mage king is coming for me, shouldn't we hear their pursuit?"

Ayden let go of my hand so suddenly, I thought I'd said something wrong. An icy breeze blew, and I shivered.

Avoiding my gaze, Ayden stood. "I feel much better," he mumbled. "Let's keep going."

I followed, a lump swelling in my throat. What had just happened? Why did I feel confused about what had passed between us?

CHAPTER 8

The rest of the day passed without mishap and we continued, our pace quickening as Ayden regained his strength. Once streaks of sunset caused the sky to blush, Ayden led me to an old, giant tree. A pile of brown and yellow leaves hugged the trunk, but Ayden brushed them away until a narrow opening appeared, wide enough to allow him to squeeze through.

I followed and found myself inside the bottom of a hollow tree. The ground beneath my feet was a combination of moss and dried, dead leaves, a sort of cushion for me to walk on. The air inside was much warmer, cozy, and I loosened my grip on my cloak, even though my body was heated from the march through the wood.

Faint light from the sunset chased away the shadows while knotted brown roots twisted up into walls. It was a clever hiding spot. Ayden sat down heavily, pressed his body into a nook and closed his eyes. Why was he so exhausted? My gaze flickered to the opening. If I were quiet, I could sneak out. The thought dropped away just as quickly, for after dark I knew not what terrors the wood held. Besides, I didn't want to escape from him, not anymore. The thought left me grumpy.

Settling down, I opened my bag to take the draught which kept me sane. As I'd walked, the edges of uncontrollable magic swirled around me, and I longed to chase them away. Holding up the bottle, I studied it, hoping there was enough elixir to last the journey. I'd have to ask Ayden if there was an apothecary or something similar near his home.

I glanced at him, but he seemed to be asleep. A few moments later there came a snuffling sound and the pile of leaves moved. My heart leaped into my throat and I stood, backing away from the entrance. A black nose burst through, followed by a whirl of white. My hand went to my chest in relief, for it was only Wilbur. His eyes glowed like a luminous light in the semidarkness.

"Wilbur," Ayden whispered, opening his eyes. He smiled as Wilbur trotted up to him, nosed at his body, then sniffed at the bandage, and growled.

With a frown, I sat back down, hugging my cloak tight. If Ayden looked at me the same way he looked at Wilbur—with care and concern—I'd be grateful. But I shouldn't think such things, I should try to find a solution to my problem. Well, Ayden's problem which he'd dragged me into so now it was my problem too. I sighed.

"Solvay?"

I glanced up, heart beating faster at the sound of my name. Ayden wasn't looking at me though, but still petting Wilbur, those long fingers moving through the fur in a fluid way.

"I'm not going to try to run away again," I told him. "Not tonight."

Ayden chuckled, the sound stirring something in my belly. "No, it's not that. Are you comfortable? We won't be able to build a fire tonight but there's dried meat and water in my pack. Help yourself. Tomorrow we'll reach the river and refill."

"Oh." His words stunned me, and for a moment I sat still, at a loss for words. "Thank you," I whispered.

His thoughtfulness made me feel even more terrible about what had happened. Ice lords were supposed to be terrible and evil. In fact, shortly after I arrived at the village, there was an incident. Animals were found outside the gate, bodies ripped open, organs removed, bodies drained of blood. The mages claimed it was the ice lords, who drank blood and used the organs for foul magic. But it didn't make sense. Ice lords didn't have magic and although they were rumored to drink blood, I hadn't seen Ayden drink anything other than water. Was it possible the villagers, nay even the mages, were wrong about them?

We left at first light, but the day was gray and cold. Ayden took us uphill and by midday my legs were burning. Ayden and Wilbur were silent companions, Ayden leading the way while Wilbur trotted behind me. Probably to keep me from running away again, not that I had the urge left. I wanted nothing more than to sit in front of a fire and enjoy a cup of chamomile tea. Did the ice lords have such comforts in their ice kingdom? Clearly not all of them had hearts made of stone.

"We're almost to the river," Ayden called. "It's rough

terrain ahead, but we'll take the secret passage, a short-cut, into the mountains."

I nodded, even though he was walking ahead of me.

He lifted his face to the sky and slowed. "Besides, it looks like snow, although I had hoped the last of the winter storms were over with."

I blanched. "What happens if it snows? We're out here, exposed."

"I know the mountain's secrets, no matter what happens, we will find a way."

His words filled me with confidence. After all, he was the ice lord, he knew the mountains best, and I was curious about the secret passage. Perhaps it would provide an ample hiding place.

As we walked, I waited to hear the rushing of water but there was none. The air grew colder, and when we reached a glittered white patch, exposed to the open, Ayden pointed. "There it is."

I stared blankly, seeing nothing except a glittering sheen of white. Wait, no, it was ice. The river was almost completely iced over, but someone had carved a hole near the shore into a perfect square.

"On my way down the mountain I took some time to fish," he explained.

I stared. "Fish? In this cold?"

He shrugged. "I needed food and some time to think. It was a productive endeavor."

"Think about what?" I bit back the words as soon as I spoke them, sure I could guess what he thought about.

A frown crossed his face before he walked down the embarkment. I stood on the shore, arms crossed, while he refilled the water skins. There was something else, I tasted it in the wind, the scent of something otherworldly. But it seemed I was the only one who sensed it. Wilbur trotted down to the river, put his muzzle in the ice and lapped up the water.

Ayden trudged back to me, squinting at my expression. "What's wrong?"

"I hear something." I studied the riverbed which wound away, twisting and curving out of sight.

He followed my gaze. "There's a waterfall down the river."

"No, something else," I breathed, sending a puff of white mist into the air.

He handed me a water skin and reached for his axe. "You didn't notice the golem, but now you sense something coming?"

Those words burned and my eyes flashed as I glared at him. A moment later, a crack came and then a babble of noise. I stiffened while Ayden laughed.

"Sit," he encouraged me, dropping in the snow. "You'll want to see this."

I scowled. It didn't seem wise to stop for long, and I didn't understand why Ayden wasn't more concerned. Reluctantly, I lowered myself down. My legs ached with relief as I stretched them out in front of me, using my cloak to shield me from the snow.

Ayden cupped his fingers around his mouth. "Wilbur, heel!"

A moment later, the air was full with the swirling of white feathers as great ice birds flew over the river. I drew in a sharp breath as they whirled. They were beautiful, their sharp beaks striking the ice, cracking it as they scooped up fish.

Underneath their white feathers were plumes of color, crimson red, royal purple and a bright, bold blue. They were as big as eagles and moved in a pattern, some wheeling over the water, others diving. Using a series of short calls, they encouraged each other. Once the first group ate, they took watch while the next group did the same.

"What are they?" I asked, entranced by their wild beauty.

"Ice birds. I often see them after the last snow. Their coming means winter will thaw, the lands will warm, and the ice birds will fly north, to colder places."

"A symbol of hope," I filled in.

I studied him while he watched the birds. His pointed ears screamed fae, yet his broad shoulders, high cheekbones and the confident way he carried himself made it clear he was an ice lord. His nose was slightly crooked, as though it had been broken once and his lips... Warmth surged through me and I tore my eyes away, preventing the thoughts I should not be thinking from dancing in my mind.

This was the closest I'd been to a man in a long time. My need to hide made me end conversations quickly and move away. Out here in the wild and lonely mountain range, it was just us. I found myself drawn to his company, curious about him. There was more to this fae ice lord than brawn, that I was sure of. "What's your home like?"

Startled, his lips parted before he gave me a half

smile. "It's beautiful, especially in the spring. My older brother, Eythin, is the thane of the Val Ether. He is fair and generous. During the winter my people dwell in the ice palace, for our halls are warm and provide shelter during the long winter snow and blizzards. Summers are better, but each year we produce less and less. The fertile ground is drying up, and the mages have cut off all trade routes. We can't survive only by labor and hunting. It is not enough."

"Why don't the people leave and go to other villages?"

"Many have, but Val Ether is our home, where we keep our traditions and customs. Should we be forced to become refugees and leave all we love behind? Should we be tossed from our home simply because of the mages?"

I could not answer his question, for I knew what it was like. Closing my eyes, I recalled the settlement, the men felling trees and building homes, the scent of cedar in the air, the laughter of the women, and running with the children. Arms held me so tightly, there was love and warmth and peace and comfort. All of it gone.

"I'm sorry," Ayden said, his voice low. "It was unkind of me to mention such things when I've taken you away from everything you know. I did not think to ask about your family, your loved ones, your cultures and traditions. I wrenched you away without thinking—"

"Don't be sorry," I snapped, standing even though my legs cried out against such movement. "We should press on before the mages find us."

CHAPTER 9

*D*ays later we arrived at the face of the mountain, a sheer wall of stone shooting upward until it touched the heavens. I stepped back and stared, eyes wide as the enormity of the mountains pressed against me like herbs being ground beneath stone. My limbs felt weak, and not just from the ascent.

Despite my soreness and exhaustion, I'd noticed the desperate clawing inside had grown dim. I wasn't certain whether it was the potion I took or the knowledge that I was away from people in the wild. If worst came to worst, the destruction, the chaos would be limited although I did not want to hurt Ayden and Wilbur, despite Ayden's unsavory purpose. I pushed that thought away, for in the mountains it was easy to forget about the threat of the mage king. Besides, it was odd. Even though I looked over my shoulder every night and every morning, I caught no sign of pursuit.

Was Ayden right? Would the mages come after us, or was it only wishful thinking? I wasn't special and important. Was there a need for the mages to brave the mountain to bring me back and punish me for dishonoring the mage king? Ayden was certain they were coming and while we kept an even pace, he never stopped to look behind. I also noticed that no matter how many footprints I left in the snow, a silent wind covered my steps with snow. And now this.

I reached up to touch the sheer face of the cliff, my fingers brushing against grooved stone, embedded with snow and dirt. "What is this place?"

Ayden's eyes gleamed as he stood tall. It was clear he was proud of the mountain, proud of his heritage. "This is the entrance to the Mountain of Ether."

"Ether," I repeated, although I didn't know what it meant. "I thought the ice palace where your brother rules is Val Ether."

"It is." Pride filled his voice. "We have reached the land of the ice lords, as you call us. We are the descendants of the great warrior, Ether. Blessed with magic from the gods, he came down to this mountain to conquer the wilds. Tales say that creatures of myth rose to fight him, to drive him away, but he would not go. One by one he defeated them, and as a reward the mountain opened its heart to him, and he dwelled here in the halls, where gold and silver and other precious gems are mined."

I opened my mouth to say how impossible the story was, but a memory of wings and fire stilled my words. Instead, I reframed my question. "Do you believe that is what happened?"

He was lost, gone in a haze of glory and battle. When he spoke again, his tone was wistful. "Storytellers say that

51

legends are truth, or at least they began that way, born out of the glory of overcoming the impossible. One whispered the tale to another, the story was told during festivals and celebrations, and whispered to children during the long, snowy days. Truth became twisted, embellished, glorified, but I believe under every tale there is a foundation of truth, an undercurrent that keeps it alive. Stories give us hope, they remind us that the darkness will fade, the snow will end, and the days of starvation will come to an end. All it takes is one person to step forward and start the chain of events that will cascade into change."

My heart leaped at his words, grasping, hoping. I wanted his belief to swallow me whole, to give me a chance, to change my darkness into light. I shifted away, not wanting him to see how his words moved me or the tears that sprang to my eyes, because I too wanted hope, a chance.

He wasn't paying any attention to me, though. His fingers traced lines in the stone as though he searched for something, but his tone was reverent as he went on. "I hope to ignite that change for my people, just like a small pile of snow, if shifted the wrong way, can cause a mighty avalanche to surge down the mountainside. I hope my actions will change the destiny of my people. The line of Ether has fallen, but I don't want it to die out or the glory of the legends that surround this mountain to fall into silence. Because once the stories stop, once the knowledge is no longer shared, the world will fall into a silent and slow death."

"Why?" I inhaled. "Why death?"

He looked at me, his eyes piercing. "Because if you take away hope and light, what is left?"

My gaze fell to the ground. I couldn't look into his crystal blue eyes and tell him I already knew what was left. And that was darkness, a deep and terrible darkness that would consume all.

I didn't hear the next words he said, for he whispered under his breath. A loud click came and the ground beneath me shook as a door appeared. Ayden pressed both hands upon it and pushed while I gawked. The door in the stone opened, exhuming a cloud of dust and dry air. I stepped back in astonishment, for the carvings in the stone were, symbols and letters, the text of an old language or a spell.

Wilbur raced inside, his claws clattering over stone, sending echoes vibrating. Ayden stepped instead, but instead of walking into shadows, he stepped into a pool of silver light. When he turned around, his smile was glorious. "Welcome to the halls of Ether."

A hum came and then a long, whistling whine.

"Get down!" Ayden shouted as an inferno heat surged toward us.

CHAPTER 10

I fell to my knees, it was hot, too hot and I wanted to crawl away, to avoid being scorched under that heat, but just as suddenly, it evaporated. From my protective hunch I dared to peek back over my shoulder and my mouth dropped open. All the breath in my body whooshed away as I stared in utter amazement. Fingers of confusion poked at me, and in the uncanny silence that followed, I stood, my jaw moving up and down uselessly.

It had been a ball of fire, spinning toward the door, and yet now it was caught, frozen in a block of ice. In the seconds that passed, the block of ice fell to the ground where it shattered, sending shards of ice spinning. The heat from the fire hissed as it dissipated. Ayden was already in motion, pushing and straining against the door while Wilbur helped. Beyond the doorway, a blur of people running toward us. Mages. They'd found us.

The lump swelled in my throat and that faint clawing returned. Without hesitation, I threw myself against the stone door and helped Ayden push it shut. It closed with a click and within moments the door faded, as though it could only be opened by magic.

"It won't slow them down for long," Ayden said, lifting his hands.

He spoke, a chant in an elder tongue. Goosebumps grew on my arms, but not from cold. This time he didn't hide what he was doing. Ice came from his fingers, coating the wall where the door had been. A puff of white came out of his mouth as he worked, his lips repeating the enchantment, sealing the barriers between the known and unknown. I was in the heart of Ether with a mage, the kind of person I'd run from, and I was in his arms.

Furiously, I racked my brain. Everything made sense now, the way the snow hid our footsteps, the death of the golem, the patch of ice I'd slipped on, and why he hadn't bound me. Ayden wasn't worried I'd run away because he had the power of the mountains at his fingertips. He wasn't just a fae or ice lord. He was an ice mage.

When he turned around, his eyes darkened at the look on my face. "No time for questions." He picked up the bag he'd dropped earlier. "We have to move."

He reached out for me, but I backed away, my heart pounding in my chest. There would be no escaping him now. My mind scrambled, trying to make sense of it all. Mages and ice lords did not mix, yet Ayden was an ice mage, dwelling in the mountains instead of the mages' castle. I wanted nothing more than to stop and think, but Ayden led the way, hurrying down the open path into the mountainside.

Wilbur trotted at my heels, ensuring I kept up, probably some unspoken bond between him and Ayden. Mages often had a link with animals to strengthen their magic. It made sense now, but threads of fear grew and that clawing came sharper, more intense.

I had to forget about it, to stop my anxiety, to calm my fears. I focused on my surroundings. An odd blue light hovered around us. It was everywhere, beneath my feet, in the stone and above my head, even though the top of that mighty hall was swallowed in darkness. Sheer walls shot up hundreds of feet into the air, the stones carved with a mix of images and words. Stone statues had been placed in corners, around curves, and stared at us, silent watchers as we dashed by.

Ayden broke into a run, and I followed. Passageways split off, descending into obscurity beyond the luminous blue glow. Should I dash down one and lose myself in the mountain? He would chase after me though, and now that I knew his secret, I wasn't sure what I should do. Originally, I thought Wilbur was the dangerous one who kept me in line, but it had been Ayden all along. I recalled the head wound I'd given him and how he reacted afterward. Magic was dangerous and always extracted a price. Was his weariness that day the price he'd paid for saving me?

Breathing hurt, my lungs cried out for a pause, a relief. I had no idea how long we went on until Ayden took a sharp turn and opened yet another hidden door. He ushered me inside and shut it. "Rest here," he whispered.

I couldn't rest, I had to know. Stumbling into the

room, I took it in one glimpse. It was clearly a place to rest with bundles and blankets and a bed. One bed. I gulped as I breathed in hard, trying to catch my breath.

"Sit," Ayden instructed.

He approached me, dropped one hand to my shoulder and, as much as I wanted to fight him, I allowed him to steer me back until I sat on the edge of the bed. It sagged under my weight but held.

"Here." He thrust a water skin into my hands. "We have maybe an hour and then we need to move again. Once we reach the pass, it will be difficult for them to cross over into the land of the ice lords."

"Because of magic?" I glared at him, ignoring the way his eyes beseeched me to believe him, to understand. "Who are you, exactly, Ayden? Are you an ice lord or a mage? Why did you truly capture me? Is everything you told me a lie because I'm not some weak woman, I can handle the truth!"

He ran a hand through his hair, mouth working. "I didn't want to frighten you."

"No?" My nostrils flared. He looked so rugged and handsome standing there, hair wild, chest heaving as he breathed. "It's too late to keep me from being frightened when you took me from everything I know—"

Much to my horror, a sob escaped my throat.

"I know," he groaned. "I know and I'm sorry. This is all wrong. I made a rash mistake. Instead of consulting with my brother, I left Val Ether and made an impulsive decision. Now I'm bringing war to the doorstep of my people. But I'm tired of sitting around, waiting for things to change. I had to take action, although I don't expect your forgiveness, it was the wrong action. Just let me help make it right."

He made it impossible to hate him. When I stood to fight him, to run away, to escape, to hide, he pulled me against his hard warm chest. It was so unexpected another sob broke free and my body quaked against his. I kept my arms by my side, fists tight, trying not to press my face into his furs, for I didn't want to return the hug, didn't want to be swept away in his embrace and his magic.

As he held me, something shifted inside, the clawing disappeared, my fingers unclenched and tentatively I brought my hands up. It had been so long since I'd allowed myself to feel raw emotion, to let go of reining in my feelings. I'd purposefully distanced myself from everyone, keeping them at arm's length, never getting too close. The awkward beginnings with Ayden had forced me to accept his help, but now my fears rose, threatening to drown me. I clung to him as if he were the only one who could save me, my finger borrowing in his furs.

My heart ached with the weight of my secret, but I couldn't tell him, even though it begged to be let out, practically bloomed on the tip of my tongue. Here in the dark halls of the mountain was the ideal place to tell him, to explain why I couldn't be the bride of the mage king. But would Ayden, with all his magic, understand my plight?

His hands dropped to my waist as he pulled back, angling his head to study my face. His inquisitive expression sent a shiver of desire down my back. A sharp awareness of what we were doing made me press my hands against his chest and step back.

With a sigh, he let go, but didn't move away. I wasn't sure if I wanted him to. "I don't know much about you, Solvay. Where you come from, what your family is like, and what you want, aside from what you don't want. A marriage to the mage king. Where were you running to when you left? Where do you want to go?"

He was so close, just a breath away. If I so much as moved, I'd be in his arms again, but I didn't deserve such comfort. He raised his eyebrows, waiting for me to speak.

When I started, the cascade of words wouldn't stop, like the flow of a river caught in a current, forced over the edge of a cliff into the falls. "That's just the problem. I'm the ideal match for the mage king. My family came from forgotten shores long ago, settling in the empire of Nomadia to rebuild, but disaster struck the settlement and destroyed them. I escaped and have been traveling alongside the lake ever since, moving from village to village, never staying long. On the day of the tithe, I should have trusted my instincts and left Lansing Falls, but I assumed the mages would ignore me, as they did previously. I'm alone in this world, and that's how it should always be. Where I go, I leave death and destruction, I'm darkness, a curse, a monster." I broke off, gasping, for his expression shifted. It morphed into confusion and then a look I could not stand. I didn't need his pity. "Don't feel sorry for me, it is my burden to bear."

He moved, threading his fingers through my hair and brushing it off my shoulder. "No, you are who you believe you are. If someone told you that you are darkness, a curse, a monster, they were wrong. You can choose who you become."

I wanted to believe him, but the memories rose, stronger than before. The claws, the blood, the teeth and the fire... Shaking my head vehemently, I backed away, breaking contact. "Like you said earlier, you don't know me at all."

As he opened his mouth to respond, a high shrieking wail pierced the air.

CHAPTER 11

"*W*hat was that?" Chills ran up my spine as the cry came again.

Wilbur whined, claws tapping on the ground as though he wished to escape.

Ayden spun, putting himself between me and the door. "The undead are awake, called by those without Ether blood, without the blessing to enter these mountains. We have to go."

Undead? Yes, I certainly wanted to get out of the mountain right away. If I had known undead rested here, I never would have come... Not that I'd had much choice though. I expected Ayden to dash to the door, instead he moved me aside. Dragging the bed away from the wall, he knelt and pushed open a small door.

"This hall is full of riddles, but it's always good to have an escape from a tight spot."

My heart melted a bit when he looked up at me, blue eyes shimmering with pride. I wanted to be angry because it was his fault we were in this situation and about to crawl through some terrible hole in the mountain to escape the undead and mages. But I couldn't. Nor did I want to admit to myself this was the most exhilarating adventure I'd had since the settlement.

With a sigh, I knelt beside him and peered into the hole. Unlike the rest of the hall, it was dark, and I had no idea what would greet me at the bottom. A company of mages? A tribe of undead with white bones and grim grinning skulls?

"Wilbur," Ayden called, as though he sensed my hesitation. "Scout it out for us."

Wilbur stepped into the tunnel without hesitation, his claws clicking down the stone. The walls weren't particularly tall or wide. Ayden would have to hunch a bit, but despite his bulk, he would fit too. Still, I didn't want to go down there. At least, not until another chilling howl came, making my blood run cold. I stepped into the tunnel, placed one hand on the wall and started walking. "The undead will not bother us?" I asked.

Ayden grunted as he pulled the bed to the wall, entered the tunnel and swung the hidden door shut.

A cloud of darkness descended. I clasped my hands over my mouth to keep the scream inside. The knowledge of the mages close by, the presence of Ayden and his unexpected words and the screams of the undead had taken me out of my comfort zone. I could handle travel and lack of sleep and hiding and running, but this was too much.

Ayden took a step, bumping into me in the dark. Instead of moving away, his hand tightened on my shoulder. "Undead do not care about the lives of the living, but this is their final resting place. Those who come with foul intent awaken them. We can sneak away while they fight the mages."

I swallowed hard and kept one hand on the wall, relieved Ayden kept his hand on my shoulder. Now was not the time for conversation, but I couldn't help asking more questions. "What about you? You're a mage. How come you aren't with them?"

Usually, I was good at holding my tongue, but my curiosity about Ayden rose, demanding answers.

"I used to be." He let go of me, and a moment later, a blue glow appeared.

I turned as best I could in the tunnel, glimpsing a blue light in his palm. Ice magic.

He touched my shoulder, encouraging me to go on and I did, grateful for the light.

"Twenty-five years ago, the mages came for the tithe. By their power of foresight, they discovered I had magic they sought, and so they took me. I was only five, frightened, scared, crying for my mother and father and brother. My parents fought for me, but the mages will have their way or else... Some died, and that was the day my people decided to move further into the mountains. They traveled to Ether and moved into the sacred ice palace where it is difficult for the mages to come. The tithe stopped, but so did the benefits of trade. We lost the privilege of living in the lower lands where the soil is fertile. We lost the blessing of the lake and the gifts it provides."

I closed my eyes against the pain in his words. He'd been ripped away from all he'd known at the tender age of five. He knew what it was like to lose everything and yet he'd gained it back. "How did you escape?"

"I did not. For five years I trained with the mages." His voice went thick with emotion. "They are cruel masters, especially to children. When I was ten, my brother came for me. My parents were killed in battle, and every day I am thankful for their sacrifice. I know why they did what they did, and one day I vowed to set my people free. They are afraid, they don't know the mages like I do, and if I don't act, they will sit in Val Ether until the snow buries them alive."

My heart wrenched at his sad tale. I didn't want to feel for him, I wanted to think only of myself and my escape. "I'm sorry—"

"Don't be sorry." He brushed my words away. "You are not to blame. I did not tell you my story so you could take the burden of responsibility upon yourself, only that you'd understand who I am."

"I understand," I agreed. "But why didn't the mages come after you?"

"They were afraid of the mountain, with good reason, and my brother timed it right. When the mages came after us, he started an avalanche, and then the winter set in. They could not come up here, and although we waited and waited, they never tried."

"So why now?"

"It's time," he sighed. "At first, we lay low, waiting for the mages to come for us, preparing for battle. Despite how the mages abused me, I'd learned from them, but magic of any kind, whether it used for good or evil, is frightening to those who don't have it. My people asked me to hide my abilities, but I used magic in secret, to help. Time passed, thoughts of revenge came and fled, and then after my wife died, I had more time to determine what hurt the mages most. They desire a powerful magic that will allow them to rule all. This is not my first attempt at getting their attention, but taking you is what I hope will impact them the most. The first time they didn't come after me because they already knew what I could do, the extent of my abilities, and the snow and rock rained down upon them. This time, they want you. I saw it in the scrying waters. Not you exactly, but the mage king's bride will have the power the mages have been seeking for decades. And if I have what the mages desperately want, they will listen to reason."

I pressed my lips together. Of course. I was a token, a tool to barter, but what frightened me more was that the mages knew about my power. My lips trembled, but I forced them to form words. "What did they say about my power?"

"So, it is true?"

I didn't like the curiosity in his tone. "What did they say?" I pressed.

"Nothing specific, you know how prophecies go. Words from a seer are layered with riddles. All they said was that the bride of the mage king would have the power the mages sought, the ability for them to rule all."

Fear choked out my anger. "Knowing this, you would hand me over to them and allow them to rule all?"

Ayden didn't answer, and I felt his conflicted heart. How I sensed it, I didn't know, but it was there. He'd asked himself this question again and again, sat out in the wild, catching fish, trying to think through what to do. Either way, he had to act, but what would be the outcome? He'd only delayed the mages, and if he turned me over to them...

My breath caught and the clawing inside built, that need to run away. Pressing a hand to my stomach, I paused to catch my breath. The clawing wouldn't stop. Scenes flashed before my mind, the settlement in flames, the screams, the blood, so much blood, running red like a river. Shredded burned flesh and eyes that ever watched, then a deep gurgling. I hissed and shook my head hard. *Make it stop. Make it stop!*

"Solvay? What's wrong?"

Sinking to my knees, I wrapped my arms around myself and rocked back and forth, a low, keening sound tearing from my throat. Had I forgotten to take the potion? I hadn't had an episode in so long. Dimly. I heard Ayden calling my name, firmly and then an edge of fright. Wilbur whined, then growled. A chilling scream came, but it was so far away. Wind rushed as my vision tunneled.

My breath came short and fast. I fought for air, fought to stop the monster from gaining control. It sapped my strength, threatening to send me back into a hellish dream. I rocked harder, sweat beaded on my head, curled around my neck and slid down my back. Soon it would begin.

"Fight it!" The shout came, and fingers of ice touched my cheek.

The beast relented just in time. Eyes blind, my fingers

fumbled in my bag. I yanked out the bottle and Wilbur growled, then barked. My fingers shook, and I dropped it.

"Here," Ayden said.

A moment later, the vial was pressed to my lips. I drank, swallowed, forcing the monster to return to sleep.

When I opened my eyes, Ayden stared at me, concern in his eyes. Shame washed through me as his brow furrowed. I needed him to understand that taking me up the mountain to his people was the last thing he should do if he truly wanted to free them from the mages. The truth formed on my lips. He'd shared his tale, and it was time for me to tell what I'd told no other living being, what grew inside me until it became too ugly, too scarred to share. Once he realized the truth, he'd let me go, and I'd return to my lonesome ways. Even though I didn't want to.

That knowledge struck me like a blow to the head, and for a moment spots danced before my eyes. Ayden's hand was on my waist, pulling me closer.

"Ayden," I breathed. "You have to know the truth."

Two luminous eyes appeared, and the words died on my lips.

CHAPTER 12

"**W**atch out," I cried, leaping to my feet.

My momentum brought Ayden with me and he spun, hand going to his axe as he shielded me with his body. A curse vibrated through him as I peered over his shoulder.

Wilbur paced and growled in front of the thing, and my skin went cold. It was a creature from a nightmare, with orb-like glowing eyes, a pear-shaped head and skin so dark it blended into the shadows. We'd reached the end of the tunnel, but instead of light, the rest of the space was a hollow of blackness. In the gloom I smelled the bite of still water and heard a slight rush, like wind blowing over a crevice.

"What is it?" I whispered.

"A bloodsucker," he replied. "They live in the gloom in the forgotten places of the mountains. I didn't know one lived down here."

"Is it going to attack?"

"Maybe..." He scratched his neck. "I don't know much about them, other than to stay away. Follow my lead."

He took a side step, following a path I couldn't see that led upward. I stubbed my toe as I followed, unaware of the incline and unwilling to drag my eyes away from that nightmarish creature.

It watched while Wilbur growled, a shield between us.

Ayden continued to sidestep until the creature moved. The eyes closed and I caught a blur of movement before the creature was upon us.

"Run!" Ayden shouted, pushing me ahead of him.

I turned up the path, my hand slapping against a wall which I followed. Behind me I heard scuffling and when I peered back over my shoulder, the blue light allowed me to glimpse Ayden chopping with his axe while Wilbur barked, encouraging him.

Shuddering, I waited, my body shaking at each slash of the axe, and the sound of it chopping into flesh. The stink of death filled the air and my stomach twisted.

"Go!" Ayden called.

But I waited until he was beside me before running into darkness.

We ran until my throat was raw, then slowed down. My back ached and my legs burned. If anything, this journey showed me I was not ready to ascend the mountain into the halls of the ice lords. How delightful it would be to lie down on a bed of furs or soak in a hot bath. Yet time dragged on, the endless passages, the dark, the blue light, and the rush of power. We left behind the screams of the undead, the threat of the bloodsuckers, and when I thought I couldn't go on any longer, Ayden took my arm. "Rest now," he whispered.

I was too exhausted to ask where we were, but I lay down on furs, the hard ground beneath me, closed my eyes and slept.

THE RUMBLING of my stomach woke me and I sat up, yawning and stretching. My hair was knotted and skin felt as if it were coated with a fine layer of grime. It was colder though, and I dragged my cloak around me, surprised it was bright enough to see. A tiny pool of sunshine poured in from a hole about a foot wide. It was high above me, and yet that light was beautiful.

After the warm darkness yesterday, it was easy to assume I'd walked in a tomb. Chewing on some smoked fish, I studied the room. It was a circular depression of stone, with runes carved into it. Ayden lay close to me and Wilbur kept watch. What a curious mountain, with hidden doors and passageways. It would be easy to be lost in here, forever.

Lost. That's exactly what I was and how I had to remain. This would be an ideal place, full of dead things and demons. Although I'd hate myself forever if I were trapped here, it also meant I couldn't hurt anyone anymore.

Closing my eyes, I let that thought drift away and wondered what it would be like if I were normal instead of a monster. Would I let myself be taken away by the mage king? According to Ayden, I was only chosen because of my power. Without the monster, I'd be free to walk among the villagers without worry. I could speak out without fear and I'd have my own shop and help others because their gratefulness was enough.

A lump swelled in my throat as the realization dawned on me. I had a choice, and the person who needed my help the most was Ayden. Opening my eyes, I looked at him as though seeing him for the first time.

In sleep, his bold and brazen looks had softened. Gone was the barbaric ice lord and in his place was just Ayden, with his long blond hair, some braided, other stands loose. Crystal blue eyes relaxed in sleep, but his lips were parted. I followed the curve of one arm tucked under his head and the other, fingers closed around his axe, ready should some intruder spring upon us.

What if he had come for me, demanded I become his bride? Would I have fled? Knowing what I knew about him now, a flush rose to my cheeks. I wanted to stay, to find out if there was something between us, something more than friendship. He may have been stolen by the mages, but he had a good heart and I trusted him.

It was that revelation that rocked my world, and I squeezed my hands into fists. So little time and yet his presence drew me toward him, even learning he had ice magic did not scare me. I wanted time to get to know him, to understand his desire to protect his people, to avenge his parents' death, to make the mages pay.

The power to destroy the mages was within me, but I couldn't go back with the mages. If they took me to their castle and I turned into the monster, I would wreck everything at the expense of innocents. The chosen brides and children of the tithe would die, and I could not have their blood on my hands. No. To prevent a war between ice lords and mages, I had to sacrifice myself and destroy my power.

The beginnings of an idea swept into my mind just as Ayden opened his eyes.

yden liked to talk, or perhaps he enjoyed talking to me. I had to admit, I'd never heard a man talk so much as we continued our ascent. "We'll arrive in Val Ether today," he told me.

The passageways were much wider, and occasionally daylight streamed in from holes far above us. The air, too, was much colder. I shivered, even in my wool cloak, and swung my arms and legs to warm them up. It helped, but not much. No wonder he wore so many furs. Cold like this, even on the brink of spring, could not be withstood for too long.

"Once we leave the mountain, there's a bridge with views of the mountainside to rival the gods themselves, and after that, a fair walk, only a couple of miles, to the ice palace. The bridge separates us from this mountain, from this great hall, but come spring we'll return to gather precious gems and craft weapons."

"There are gems in the mountain?" I asked, watching

the light in the walls shimmer. It was odd but welcoming, I felt calm watching it.

Ayden laughed. "Of course, it's a mountain, a great mine, a forge, a tomb, life revolves around Ether."

"It's a fortress," I added. "And a hiding place. How can you stand coming here with the mix of unsavory creatures within? Like the bloodsucker?"

"I admit you glimpsed the darker side of Ether, the bowels of the mountain. If the mages hadn't found us, I would have taken you through the sacred route, through the halls of warriors and the throne of kings. It is a sight well worth it. The tombs are that way, sacred and magnificent. I need a second journey to show you the glory of the mountains. What you've seen is nothing in comparison."

I wanted to tell him there wouldn't be a return journey, instead I said, "I'd like to see it."

His eyes warmed, and his lips curled back into a smile. A pleasant glow spread across my chest and my finger tingled. If something as simple as a smile made me feel this way, I couldn't imagine how more of him would influence me.

We rounded a bend and white light poured in. Daylight. A series of wide stone steps led up to a platform, and above it, a door stood wide open. Light danced around it, flecks of white and blue. My jaw dropped as I stared. The legends were true, there were wondrous sights to behold.

Ayden paused, letting me take it in. Beside the doorway were alabaster columns and stone statues of beings I'd never seen. They were roughly fifteen feet tall with heads like a wolf, long tails like a cat, and sharp ears like an elf. Fae could be the only term for them. They held spears in their hands and under each foot was a scroll. Wings shot out from their backs, creating the archway over the door. I tilted my head back to stare. "Who are they?"

"The creators of the mountains. They protect the heart. In ancient days, there was a pestilence that struck the land with death. Finally, a knight climbed the mountain to ask the gods to deliver them, and tales say that with him walked a great warrior. They battled the mountain to reach the gods, and because of their valor the mountains were open to all and the pestilence ended. Now, when you walk through the gates, it is because the gods have seen your struggles and grant you access to the lands beyond."

All his stories spoke of struggle and loss, only to find a place of hope and help. "You are full of legends," I told him.

Pivoting, he stood in front of me, so close I was forced to tilt my head to meet his gaze. "And you are full of mystery." His tone was husky. "What is it you were going to tell me before the bloodsucker interrupted?"

I closed my eyes, unwilling to look at him. Everything about him was distracting and made me want what I could not have. Here in the daylight, within these hallowed walls, the past darkness seemed nothing but a bad memory, a terrible nightmare. I hadn't had an episode in years. Was it possible that I could tamper down my monster and walk in the light?

"It's about the mages. You said they saw my power?"

"Aye, a great power." His brow furrowed. "You know what it is, don't you?"

I shook my head. "I need you to understand that it is not a power that can be harnessed or used. I'm not what they think I am, who you think I am."

He pressed his lips together, eyes searching mine. "What are you saying? That you're not... human?"

Human. That word was often used, for most of the villagers were human, the ice lords were fae and the mages were a combination of all, their magic the unifying bond between them.

"No, not human," I confirmed. "My people came from across the water to this land, a new settlement, a place to start over without the demons. I know nothing about the place other than what they shared with me. I was young back then, but I remember clearly. We fled from demutos who could change their skin to look like my people, but they were monsters. They'd slip into the midst of the people, walk like them, talk like them, gain their trust, and then lose control. When they did, they went into a sort of frenzy and destroyed everything and everyone. The demutos took over the land, and the living had to flee."

I took deep breaths. I'd never told anyone that story and what came next was even more horrible. For a moment I wanted to run, to put it all behind me.

Ayden touched my shoulder. His voice was low. "Did your people fight? Surely they discovered the weakness of the demutos?"

"They did, but it was too late to take back their land, so they left. One of my uncles discovered the remedy, garlic and cloves or ginger used in a varying degree can keep the demutos calm, keep them from lashing out and losing control."

Ayden's eyes dropped to my bag and my potion, the combination of garlic and ginger mixed with cinnamon making it bearable to swallow.

"Do you believe you're one of them?"

Emotion rose so thick it closed my throat. I couldn't look at him. I couldn't speak. I gave a slight nod. Tears blurred my eyes as I recalled the frenzy, losing control, and waking up covered in blood. No one was left alive, not the hundred that had come, taking such precautions to ensure we all survived. I recalled taking that odd mixture. It tasted bad, but we were required to drink it. My mother had called it medicine to cleanse us from the old world. To cleanse the blood of darkness. Grown up, I knew better. Nothing could cleanse the blood from that kind of darkness. It was always with me, haunting my steps, stealing my happiness.

"Solvay." He moved closer. "Why do you tell me this now? I've watched Lansing Falls for years, I've ventured to other villages and I've never heard of an incident where an unnamed creature attacked. Are you sure?"

I paused, my thoughts going back to memories I'd repressed. There'd always been the clawing inside, but I had no memory of a different form other than the skin I was familiar with. Ayden's question forced me to consider something else. My early memories were so hazy I always assumed, because of my knowledge of the demutos and the medicine we all took to keep from changing, that I had been the cause. But then how would I explain the clawing inside? The knowledge that if I didn't calm myself, everything would shatter, and I'd fly into a bloody frenzy.

It had only happened once, but since then I'd been careful, so careful. There were days when everything blurred into darkness, when I was traveling, but I didn't know whether it was from exhaustion or a shift. Still, the fact that it could have been nothing was too good to be true. "I feel it within me," I told him, lifting my chin. "I won't let it out."

Instead of protesting or asking more questions, he nodded, and his shoulders sagged. "Now I understand why you fled, why you don't want to go back. Even a hint of that power in the hands of the mages will be danger-ous. They take magic and shift it, twisting it to meet their desires. They take something innocent and turn it evil, just to brag about their power, their dominion, their magic. To rule and conquer, to inspire fear means they achieve their goals. I would not see them use you in such a way, regardless of what kind of power you may carry."

"But what will you do?" I protested. "Your people need help; you have to make a deal with the mages."

"I know," He frowned. "Come, while it is light. We will speak with my brother and come up with a solution."

I didn't know how to respond to his kindness, his will-ingness to help, especially to rectify his mistake in capturing me, and so I said nothing. Together we walked to the stairs and ascended while the giant statues stared straight ahead, granting us access to the land beyond the Hall of Ether. I glanced back when we reached the top, still awed at the magnificence of that place, and intimidated. The bluish glow hovered in the air and Wilbur growled.

When I faced forward, more blue filled my vision. Gasping, I took a step back as three blue monsters frowned down at us.

CHAPTER 14

*A*yden groaned as he reached for his axe. "Frost giants? Here?"

I couldn't tear my eyes away from them, for I'd never seen such beings. Giant was correct, for they were all at least eight feet tall with bare arms and legs with corded muscles. One blow would lay me out flat. They wore threadbare clothes which slowed off their muscled chests and other body parts I did not wish to see. One had shaggy hair rippling down to its shoulders, another had a crown of white hair that stuck up straight in the air, and the third was bald.

Their faces were set in deep scowls and whatever strength and confidence I had faded. I fully expected Ayden to suggest we run back into the halls of Ether, but he twirled his axe in his hands. "I'll distract them while you run for it. We have to get to the bridge, if we reach it, we can escape."

The bridge? What bridge? But when I looked beyond the frost giants I saw it. A crystal bridge arched into the air, sparkling as it crossed the void, before sinking down to the other side of the mountain. Val Ether. Ayden's home. It may have been a trick of the air, but I could have sworn I saw the pinnacle of an ice palace, sparkling in the sunshine.

I took a deep breath as the frost giants charged. Ducking off the platform by the gates of Ether, I fully intended to run toward the bridge. My foot sank into deep snow, up to my shins. Cold crept through my boots, numbing my feet. I took another step, trapping my other foot. I struggled, but the giants approached fast. The white-haired one reached out a hand to knock me over or snatch me up, I didn't know which and I did not have a weapon. I did the only thing I could think of. Quickly, I snatched up snow and packed it into a ball before hurling it.

It smacked into the side of the giant's face and he froze, then threw back his head and roared. It took me a moment to realize it was laughter, and I couldn't blame him. It was pathetic to think a snowball could do much against frost giants. Despite the odds, I took advantage of his distraction and darted around him. The snow was packed and thicker as I moved toward the bridge, and behind me I glimpsed Ayden fighting.

Eyes wide, I slowed. He lunged with his axe, his face a mask of fury as he roared and darted between the giant's legs, bringing his axe up with a thrust that sent blood spurting. I swallowed hard as he drove the axe into the back of the giant, felling it with multiple blows to its back and legs. When a second frost giant swung at him, he ducked and brought his free hand up, sending a spear of ice into its chest. He followed it up with a series of blows and advanced on the third giant who turned to run.

Ayden gave chase while I watched in horror. This barbaric display was exactly what I expected from the ice lords. The way he swung the axe followed by his furious slashes and ice magic made him invincible. If he were cornered, he could take on an entire army. I edged back, for this was my chance to escape. Memory flashed in my mind, the blood, the screams, the taste of iron in my throat, running until the soles of my feet were blackened and ripped.

I made for the bridge until Wilbur's sharp barks and a rumbling made me turn around. Five more ice giants appeared from behind a rock and advanced. Ayden pivoted on his heel and a spray of ice exploded from his fingertips, diving like darts into the faces of the ice giants. He ran toward me, blood streaking his face and furs. "Make for the bridge!" he shouted.

Wilbur bounded ahead of me, growling, then paused at the foot of the bridge, waiting for me to cross. My pulse thumped hard and my legs burned as I forced them through the thick snow, fighting to gain speed. Wilbur's tracks helped somewhat until I reached the smooth edges, my fingers grasping the rails of the bridge.

It was a beautiful creation, wide enough for five or six men on horses to pass through. It stretched over a gaping void that tunneled down, and somewhere below came a faint rumble, like thunder. White mist rose on either side and I ran up the sloping bridge, daring myself not to look back. When I reached the center of the bridge, it trembled beneath my feet.

Glancing over my shoulder, I glimpsed Ayden behind me, but he slowed to a stop and whirled as the frost giants pounded over the bridge toward us, making it shake. There were too many of them and my heart dropped. Unless Ayden's magic could stop them, they'd catch us. Ayden uttered a curse and lifted his hands. "Go," he shouted, and suddenly the air was full of snow. It rained down upon us, a beautiful mist.

Spinning around, I lost my footing and slipped. My hands flew out to catch my fall, but I went down hard, my shoulder taking most of the impact. I cursed. Sitting up gingerly, I felt my shoulder. Each touch sent shards of hot fury across my skin. I lifted my bag off my shoulder to relieve the misery.

Behind me, the frost giants beat their clubs on the bridge, shouting and growling as they neared. Clutching my arm to my side, I lurched to my feet and forced my feet to move, ignoring the pain that made tears press against my eyes. Dimly, I heard Wilbur's sharp barks and Ayden cry out.

I twisted as a ball of fire hovered in the air and then exploded on the back of a frost giant. It howled and threw itself to the ground, trying to beat out the pain.

Fire...

My eyes widened as men strode out of the gates of Ether. No, not men. Mages. I was too far away to see them clearly, but as they lifted their hands, a shimmering began in the air. The wind howled, bringing their murmured chant to my ears. They were going to cast a spell, and I'd be back with them, forced to marry the mage king while they experimented on me to discover my power.

My chest tightened. Ignoring the pain in my shoulder that increased with each jarring step, I fled. All the while, a knowing pricked inside me. Crossing the bridge would not stop the mages or bring me peace. My troubles would only arrive on the doorstep of the ice lord's haven. This was wrong, all wrong. In order to save them I had to act, and the only action would be to turn around, walk across that bridge, dodge the frost giants and give myself to the mages.

My bag snagged on the railing. Using both hands, I yanked at it as the bridge shook. Ayden was close, his eyes wild. He looked like a madman, bloody axe in his hand as he reached the midpoint of the bridge and sprinted toward me. "I'm going to break it," he shouted. "I have to take it down. It's the only way to stop the mages!"

Lifting his axe above his head, he slammed it down into the bridge. I expected nothing to happen. After all, what was an axe to a bridge? But Ayden lifted his hands, speaking words into the wind. Magic.

The bridge swayed, and a ball of flames flared above us. Reaching out a hand, Ayden stopped it with ice.

My bag was still tangled. I tugged one more time, and it split open, half of it coming loose into my hands. The other half, with all the contents, spilled over the side of the bridge. I stared in horror, my throat constricting as my bottle of potion slipped into the void. I dropped the remains of the bag, unable to take in what had just happened.

The bridge shook again, and a cracking sound filled

the air. Ayden's hand on my back propelled me forward, and I ran as the ground cracked beneath my feet.

The bridge snapped and rumbled, sending a cloud of dust into the air. Suddenly I pitched forward and fell face first into a bed of fresh snow. It cushioned my fall but didn't stop me from crying out as the impact jarred my arm. Rolling over, I watched as the crystal bridge shattered and dropped into the void.

On the other side, the frost giants turned on the mages who fought them with magic. I scrambled away, panic setting in. My potion was gone, it was only a matter of time until I discovered whether I was a demuto or if I had imagined it all.

When I turned to face Ayden, he wasn't with me. I spun around and spied him at the edge of the cliff, lying face down in fresh snow. "Ayden?" I called, my voice cracking, but he didn't move.

My heart stilled as Wilbur nudged him, then looked at me, eyes sad, begging me to do something.

"Ayden?" I stumbled toward him, my entire body trembling because I didn't want to be the cause of yet another death.

CHAPTER 15

"*A*yden." I held back a sob as I crawled to him and shook his shoulder. He'd taken off his furs at some point and my hand lay flat on leather. He was still warm, and I tried to push him over, but he was too heavy.

When he lifted his head, relief slammed through me so hard I almost wept. Wilbur, echoing my emotions, whined. I sat down, not caring that the snow soaked through my cloak. "Oh Ayden, are you wounded?"

He blinked snow off his eye lashes and groaned. Pressing a hand to his side, he rolled onto his back and took a deep breath. "Too much magic," he wheezed. "It took my strength."

I glanced back at the gap between us and the mages. "You've stopped them for now."

"Momentarily. They will find a way across. They will come." He took another breath, gathering his strength. "We need to reach Val Ether before they figure out how to cross. At the very least they will be upon us in the morning."

Morning? It was too soon. Not enough time to plan or prepare, and worst of all, my potion was gone. By tomorrow I'd feel the effects. There was only one action to take. I sat there in the snow with Ayden, my spirits sinking lower.

He forced himself up, grimacing as he did so, and that's when I saw the blood that stained his side. "You are wounded," I gasped.

"I'll be fine," he grunted.

I stood to my feet, clutching my arm to my chest, and together we set off through the snowdrifts.

It was cold, and the journey seemed much longer than a mere two miles. My anxiety eased when a glimmer formed into the pinnacle of an ice palace, built into a cliff. A path twisted up toward it, zigzagging back and forth. I imagined up there one could see for miles. It was a fortress, a city built into the mountainside with blue and white towers, taking on the shape and form of giant icicles.

"This is home?" I whispered, staring at it. "It's beautiful!"

"Indeed," he said, his voice thick with pain.

Our pace slowed further as we ascended. A hush hung in the air and snowflakes whirled about us. At first, I assumed it was magic, but it was actually snowing, a gentle, steady flow leaving flakes in my hair and soaking the hem of my cloak. Soon I hoped there would be a roaring fire and a warm bath.

Ayden paused just before we reached the gates and a high wall that led into the dark opening of the palace. "Solvay, you should know a few things before we enter."

I faced him, looking up into his eyes, clouded with pain and remorse. He clenched his jaw, took a deep breath and continued. "Before I left, I argued with my brother as he didn't agree with my plan. I must go to him first and explain myself, then we shall rest. My brother is thane here because he is wiser than I, and he might have a solution we haven't considered yet. Time runs short, but I want you to know I will help you. It's the least I can do after taking you away."

He sighed and lifted his eyes to the gates.

"Ayden," I hesitated, wanting to reach out and bridge the gap between us, to touch his chest and feel that closeness like I'd felt when I explained my past to him. A yearning rose within, making me long for a life I could never have. But I couldn't tell him that. Instead, I said, "I'm not angry with you. I don't know where I would have gone when I fled Lansing Falls, and it turns out this journey has helped me escape. So, let's go meet your brother."

We passed through the gates into a hall, our steps echoing as we entered. The aura of sacredness hung heavy and when the doors opened, the fragrance of vanilla, winter berries and lavender filled the air. A man with a crooked nose and piercing eyes strode toward us, blond hair flowing down his shoulders. A thick beard hid his expression, but he moved with resolve and a question in his eyes. Beside him were two other men. They all had the same bulk, pointed ears, thick beards and long hair. Ice lords.

"Ayden, by the gods," the blond man swore as he

grabbed Ayden's arm. "Where have you been? Don't answer that, you look terrible."

I assumed the man was his brother, and I stepped back as his eyes met mine, then narrowed as he glanced back at his brother. "What have you done?" He turned to one of the men by his side. "Send for ale, let Adelle know we have a guest."

The man bowed and strode away.

"Eythin," Ayden gripped the man's arm. "This is Solvay. I will tell you about her and why she has come with me. May we have a private word?"

"Tell me you didn't do anything foolish," Eythin frowned.

Ayden scratched his head and shrugged. "You know me, brother."

"That I do." Eythin directed his next words to me. "I hope he behaved himself out there."

I gave him a slight nod, unsure how he'd react when he heard the entire story.

We were escorted through the halls and I gazed in astonishment, wondering if the mage halls were like this. Whoever had built the ice palace had taken great time to make the inside beautiful. It told its own story similar to Ether Mountain. The walls appeared as though they were made of glass and shimmered with a blue light. When I grew closer, I saw images and words chipped into them, a story I wanted to know if I could trace my fingers across it.

We passed into a section that seemed homier where murals were painted across the wall and statues on the ceiling looked down at us. The ice lords were proud of their beginnings and heritage. It reminded me of my people, sorry to leave their land but willing to start over, carrying their knowledge. My heart sank the further we walked, solidifying my goal. I knew what I had to do.

CHAPTER 16

*F*ruity notes of ale hovered on my tongue, warming my body as I sank down on a bench outside of the room where Eythin and Ayden were talking. Ayden had asked me to wait while one of the fae brought us steaming mugs of ale. Slowly, the numbness faded from my fingers and toes as I drank. The pain in my shoulder had calmed to a throbbing ache, telling me it was only bruised, not broken. Weariness lingered in each muscle as I took another sip, then leaned my head against the wall and closed my eyes.

Odd how quickly my life had changed in a week. For the first time I'd been open, exposed, and nothing terrible had happened. Thoughts of the future rose, and I pushed them away as raised voices drifted from behind the door.

I pricked my ears, knowing I shouldn't listen in, but I couldn't help it. Eythin and Ayden's voices were distinct as they argued.

"You did what?" Eythin demanded. "It's bad enough

that you've been spying on the mages, but you stole the mage king's bride and now they're at our doorstep?"

To his credit, Ayden kept his voice level. "I know I acted impulsively and without your blessing, but how long are we going to hide up here while our people suffer?"

"You know the answer to that question, you know what happened the last time we fought the mages yet you will not relent. They will crush us with their magic and you don't have the strength to fight them. We might be superior in battle but not when magic is involved."

"That's why I brought her—"

"Against her will as a hostage?" Eythin interrupted. "Do you think the mage king will be happy to have her back? Nay, they will punish us too. You cannot trust them!"

"It's why I came to you, for a solution. We have something they want and I saw in the waters the great power they desire. Don't forget I've been in their halls, I know what they are like."

"Aye, vindictive and evil. Ayden, I know you acted with the best intentions, but this is wrong."

A beat of silence passed before Ayden spoke again. "There's more. The frost giants attacked us outside the gates of Ether. I broke down the bridge to keep them away from us, but I fear they are coming. If they are in this part of the land, what other foul beasts will come this way? Winter has been hard on all of us, but think of the creatures, winter was tough for them too, and now they come sniffing at our door. We have to do something about them too."

"It's never one problem at a time, trouble comes all at once."

"Aye, but I have an idea." Ayden's voice dropped lower.

I strained to hear, but a movement in the hall pulled my attention away. Opening my eyes, I stared up at a female fae. She wore thick furs and her hair was pulled back in a single braid she wore over one shoulder. "You must be Solvay."

"Yes." I rose.

She waved her hand. "Don't get up on my account. I'm Adelle, Eythin's wife. I understand you'll be a guest here for a time."

"Please don't go out of your way, it is only for a short time," I protested, recalling Ayden's words about the struggles of his people, the lack of food and trade. I didn't want them to do extra work on my behalf.

"Nonsense." She smiled, her brown eyes sparkling and lines around her mouth sunk into dimples. "Guests are welcome in these halls, especially guests of Ayden." She arched her eyebrows as though there were more. "He's been restless, difficult after his wife died, and it's good to see he's found someone," she went on. "I'm sure you'll want a hot bath after all that travel, I'll personally see that your room is ready."

"Oh... I... Wait, I'm not here because of..." I stammered as Adelle put her hand to her lips.

"No need to tell me, I'll keep your secret." She winked and moved away.

Oh, the timing. If only I'd heard what Ayden and Eythin were planning! She strode down the hall, head held high, powerful and confident in her movements. I doubted she ever had to consider her place in life and whether she might be a monster.

I finished my ale as she disappeared and the door opened. Ayden walked out and there were dark circles under his eyes. Our journey had taken its toll on him too.

"Solvay." He sat down, shoulders hunched. "I'm sorry to keep you waiting. I'll escort you to your room. You should rest and this evening we can discuss the plan."

I touched his hand, my fingers grazing the runes on his arm. "You should rest too," I told him, "and have someone look at your side."

A small smile tugged at the corners of his mouth. "As you command."

But he didn't move. His fingers slowly laced around mine. When he bent his head toward me, the blue in his eyes had turned dark, revealing a hunger, a need. "I'm sorry for making a mess of things, but I also can't be too sorry, because I met you. There's something about you that calls to me. I want to help you. I want you to be free to choose."

My skin tingled where he touched it, and I licked my lips. Drawn by an intoxication I dared not name, I leaned forward, taking slow, shallow breaths, as if any wrong movement would stop my forward motion.

When his lips brushed mine, my eyes closed. I couldn't help the whimper that lay in my throat as I sank into bliss. My skin went hot as though a fire blazed within. Parting my lips, I allowed him to take possession of my mouth, as though his kiss would save me, would halt the beast inside.

He was the first to pull back, a soulful expression on his face. Instead of letting go of my hand, he brushed strands of hair away from my face. "If this is what you want, we have a lot to figure out," he teased.

Regret shattered my euphoria. Standing, I tugged my hand out of his. "We should rest."

"Don't be sorry." He stood, voice husky. "I fight for what I want and I choose you."

Conflicted thoughts warred within. I wanted him too, for he was the epitome of everything I desperately longed for, a normal life. But as long as the demon lurked within, I'd never have a normal life. I'd never have him. Dipping my head so he wouldn't see the disappointment on my face, I took his arm.

Without another word, he guided me to a room, opening the door to a roaring fire, a streaming tub of water, and furs covering the floor.

He lingered at the door while I stared in surprise.

"I'll come for you later," he promised.

"You won't leave Wilbur to guard me?" I teased.

"Not this time." His eyes were soft and his gaze flickered between my eyes and lips, torn.

I wanted one kiss, a final goodbye, but when he stepped back, I knew it was for the best. I shut the door and leaned against it, eyes closed as tears streaked my face.

The clawing was back, and it was growing stronger.

CHAPTER 17

The steaming water called to me, begging me to forget about my plans, to forget about what I had to do and give myself a chance to live a normal life. I leaned against the door for a long time, torn between two desires. I knew what I had to do, I'd always known, and if I got into the tub, I'd never leave. The ale had warmed my body and the ache in my shoulder had dulled.

Unfastening my damp cloak, I crossed the room, ignoring the bed piled high with layers of fur to pull on the dry cloak that had been left for me. Enveloped in warmth, I went again to the door and cracked it open. Silence met my ears, and I slipped out, pulling the hood over my head.

Voices echoed down the hall but I turned my back to them and hurried away, retracing my steps, fingers crossed I wouldn't meet anyone. I stepped as lightly as I could until I found a door. I'd seen it when we entered and now I slipped out, back into the snow. The temperature had dropped, and it was colder. The light snow still rained down, enough, I hoped, to hide my footsteps.

Those first few moments I moved fast, trying to keep from glancing back over my shoulder to see if I was followed. Going downhill was much easier, and from there I had choices. Another path snaked upward, past the ice palace and deeper into the unknown. I took that path and ran through the snow, stumbling over patches as I moved.

Tears squeezed out of my eyes, and I gasped, hand on my heart. It hurt as if something were squeezing it and the clawing was stronger, growing rapidly. I had to put as much distance as I could between myself and the fae. I would not be responsible for their demise.

Snow circled me like wide open arms of white, welcoming me into their midst. If I did not find shelter soon, I'd freeze. But that didn't seem as terrible now that my body was chilled through. I could not feel my fingers or toes, but I pressed on while the flames of sunset shot across the sky and the depths of darkness surged. The stars came out, bright and hallow, and the fullness of the two moons of Nomadia gazed upon me, providing enough light for me to continue.

Trees appeared, a line between me and the wind. I moved into them with a grateful heart, the scent of pine heavy. It was darker under the boughs, but I kept walking, no longer following a trail, lost in the bliss of winter.

It was better this way, I kept telling myself. Better that Ayden never saw me at my worst. Now that my power was lost to both sides, the mages and ice lords could not make a deal. One should not use the power of death, and that's all I was, death walking.

My thoughts drifted as I continued. When snow whirled, icy fingers touched my skin, but I did not feel them. A hint of vanilla and winter berries hung only to be swept away by the howling wind. My vision was blurry, but I did not know whether it was from the wind and snow or my own tears.

At last, my feet refused to move, and my arms were frozen by my sides. I sank down under a tree, pressing my back against it, and waited for the monster to escape.

This is what the animals did when they knew it was their time. They limped away, broken, and went away to be alone, and wait, in solitude, for the end. The clawing was at its strongest, like a newborn bird breaking out of an egg. It ripped and tore, breaking flesh. My breath came short and fast, and for a moment the numbness gave way to sensations. It was warm, so warm. All I needed to do was close my eyes and let it take me.

I did not know the exact moment it happened, but as warmth shrouded me, lost and alone, under its wings of protection, my lucidity deepened to another level. Small things I'd missed became clear, like the milk-white moonlight reflecting off the snow. It glimmered under the light, turning shades of blue and a pale peach. Tiny icicles hung off the trees providing an endless supply of water for the faeries of the mountain, if there were any.

The silent hush that increased my fear wasn't silent at all, only a friendly quiet, allowing creatures of the day to slumber in peace. Still, I picked up faint noises, the high-pitched whine of a winged beast, the flutter of velvet wings, the soft clumps of snow that gave way under the weight of movement. I wasn't alone but surrounded by peace, the unending cycle of life that I was blessed to be part of.

A stream of events flashed before my eyes and I watched, unsure whether I was actually seeing it or if it was all a figment of my imagination.

A ship rocked beneath my bare feet. I stood, arms crossed. A hand rested on my shoulder, bony fingers squeezing as they waited. I tasted salt on my lips, so dry they cracked and bled. Suddenly there were shouts of joy, relief. Father tossed me in the air and settled me on his shoulder, then kissed mother. Home.

YELLOW FLOWERS GREW in the wood and I picked them one by one, enjoying the sharp flavor, but it was their leaves, they were important. A cry rang out. My heart thumped in my chest as I dashed out of the covering into wild grass. Hands caught me, squeezed, then pressed something to my lips. "They found us. Drink and you shall be saved." The bitter taste soured my belly and hands rubbed my back. Fear.

THE SWEET NOTE of a bell rang out, followed by a cheer. White flowers blew in the breeze. My hair was loose around my shoulders, a dress spinning around my knees. Hands clapped, a stringed instrument played and my feet tapped in rhythm, dancing around the bonfire on the beach. Embers floated above

me and someone took my hand, laughing as they pulled me in a circle. I was spinning, breathless. Happy.

A SCREAM CHOKED *with fear snapped me awake and I fought blindly in the dark, kicking away the covers. I tumbled down the ladder and dashed to the main room. "The medicine didn't work. They are among us." Warm hands guided me away to a cool, crisp night. The scent of lavender hung in the air, and then a ball of fire exploded.*

A rain of sand and dirt hailed down on us as we ran, then claws ripped, teeth snapped and soulless eyes stared into mine. A pink tongue snaked out, dripping with venom. Screams echoed, rivers of blood streamed and then hands grabbed my shoulders, shaking me. "Run Solvay, don't let them catch you!"

Fingers dug into my back and pushed, sending me whirling, stumbling, crying. In my tears I missed the cliff and I tumbled, only to be caught by the powerful updraft of wings and the bellyaching roar of a monster.

I was that monster.

The memory faded just as quickly, but I already felt the shift. When I looked down, claws had replaced my feet, covered in scales and shimmering in the moonlight, silver and blue. I hunched on all fours and arched my back, howling as my bones shifted and cracked, sliding into a new formation.

It hurt, a sudden sharp and swift pain that made me realize I was very much alive. My heart pounded in my chest and something sprouted from my back and moved. Trees poked me and when I looked down, the ground was much further away than it should have been. I took a step, and the ground shook under my monstrous legs and my claws scooped up handfuls of snow. I spread my wings, knocking into trees as I moved.

Panic set in because I was the monster, and I was fully conscious and terribly hungry. I spun, trapped in the forest, thoughts of food surging through my mind. The hunger, that's all there was, the need to feed. It blurred through my mind and I thrashed, sucking in air until I was free of the entanglement of trees.

Spreading my wings, I lifted into the air, unable to feel the frigid wind. I blinked, but my eyelids protected me from the snow. The moon, although bright, did not make up for the fact that I could see as clear as day. I whirled higher into the air and spun in a slow arc, stretching out my wings.

Something small and black flew past me, and without a thought I lashed out, catching it in my jaws and chomping down. It crunched between my teeth and I swallowed. Another creature flew out, and I snatched it up. It gave a tiny squeal and something moved beyond the edges of my vision. Arching my neck, which seemed long like a lizard's, I looked back down at the mountainside.

A shape stood in a snowbank, staring up at me, and I thought I heard someone shouting my name.

I had a name.

"Solvay! Solvay!"

An ache began in my chest and I beat my wings harder to escape. I remember that mournful cry, and I recalled what came out of me. Fire and ice slithered out

101

of my throat along with the deep knowledge that I hadn't tried to destroy them. I'd tried to save them, but I hadn't been strong enough.

I soared as the memories came back to me. The truth was within me, but I had to pass through the shadow of death, into the realm of darkness to find it. I'd assumed I was the cause because the trauma had been too much. My mind could not take it in aside from the knowledge they were gone. Dead.

I'd gone back, walked among the bodies, searching, hoping. But there was no hope, I was the lone survivor of a massacre, and the knowledge shaped my entire life. I'd forced myself to be lonely, to dwell in solitude, to never let anyone get too close. My reasoning was based on guilt. I was alive. They weren't.

The revelation struck me and I threw back my head and roared, sending a spurt of ice out of my mouth. The person down below continued to shout. I knew that voice. It was Ayden, but why he'd come after me I did not understand. I was supposed to leave him to his doom, to make a deal, and yet, he'd discovered my secret. No matter where I went or how I tried to run from him, he was right there, chasing after me. He believed in me, enough to see me in my monstrous form and come after me anyway.

I wanted to land, but I was frightened of myself and my power. I did not know how to turn back into myself, back into the Solvay whom Ayden knew. But I couldn't stay in the air all night, flying in circles.

Part of me wanted to fly away, and the other part of me wanted to stay. I'd run my entire life, and now that I knew the truth about what happened to the settlement, I wanted to know what would happen if I stayed.

Pivoting, I glided toward the ground, hesitant. All my fear rose within me as I landed, sending a puff of snow into the air. Most of it landed on Ayden, and when my vision cleared he stood on a rock, staring up at me.

CHAPTER 18

a moment passed as we stared at each other, then he lifted a hand and stretched it out. "You're Solvay, aren't you?"

I bowed my head, flaring my nostrils a little, but stayed where I was, unwilling to frighten him. I didn't know whether I could speak in this form, nor did I want to try. I simply waited.

"This is what you were afraid of turning into." It wasn't a question so much as a statement. He stepped off the rock, taking a tentative step toward me, both hands outstretched. "May I approach?"

I bowed my head again, finding it easy to nod. The shape of my face had changed. Even without seeing my reflection, I knew I had a long snout, eyes on the side of my head and scales.

Ayden stopped when he was an arm's length away, awe and reverence clear on his face. "Do you know what you've transformed into? You're an ice dragon, Solvay, not a demuto. But I see how your talents would be misused in the hands of the mages. You're not going with them because you're free. You can fly away now and choose your own fate."

Mages. Yes. That's why I'd come up the mountain, fleeing to escape from them. But what was he saying? Did he want me to fly away without helping him resolve the conflict between the ice lords and the mages? And then there were the people of Lansing Falls, giving their maidens and children to the tithe, to a treaty built on a lie.

The ice lords would not swoop down and murder the villagers in their beds. In fact, the mages in their lust for power had divided the people, forcing them to think the worst when there was no reason why they could not dwell with the fae in harmony, each benefiting from each other. I could fly away, but not away to choose my own fate for this was my second chance. Before I was a child and I couldn't save them all, but now I knew exactly what to do.

Moving my head forward, I pressed it against Ayden's palm. Warmth radiated from him and he took a sharp breath. "Solvay, you're not a monster," he whispered. "You're magnificent."

The film over my eyelids went foggy, and I blinked, then slowly moved my body, turning to the side and pressing my belly against the ground. I waited, peeking back over my shoulder at Ayden and huffing. His lips curled, and he raked a hand through his hair. "Do you want me to ride on your back?"

When I nodded, his grin widened. "I have a feeling tonight is the night for the impossible to become possible."

He slid onto my back, tucking his legs up and squeezing. When I was sure he was secure, I spread my wings and leaped. We bound into the air and I hovered, gliding before beating my wings again. I flew in a circle, testing my strength while Ayden shouted, unable to hide his exhilaration.

I wheeled us around, taking us back toward the ice palace. My senses had changed and now I picked up the thread of warm bodies and cold stone. There were other creatures in the wood, most hiding, aware of a great presence.

I HADN'T COME AS FAR up the mountain as I assumed, for there was the ice palace, yellow lights twinkling in the somber silence. Beyond was the gaping void where the bridge had been and a fire. The mages.

I aimed toward them, my belly boiling. I was going for the people of Lansing Falls, for the women who'd been taken without a choice, and the children who cried at night for their mothers and fathers.

I was going to save myself and, most importantly, I was going to give Ayden his chance at revenge. I imagined few had his strength of mind to put the past behind him and live, to seek revenge, to help his people. He had been a brave child and suffered under the wrong hands, only to have his parents die to free him.

I did not know that pain, but I'd lost everyone and everything, even parts of my sanity. It was only through Ayden's misguided deed that I knew who I was again, that I wasn't the pestilence that killed my people. I was a survivor and I would do what survivors did.

The flight to Ether Mountain paled compared to walking. The trudge through the snow had taken more of my energy than I imagined, yet now the mountain rose, desecrated by the mages. My impulse took over, and I swooped near, taking pleasure in their shouts as they knocked each other over, trying to get out of the way. One mage stood still, staff in hand, and started shouting out an incantation.

I reared my head back and a stream of ice belched out of my mouth and smote their fire. I roared as the ice crushed the embers and mages fled. However, the one with the staff stood tall, speaking, and a wave passed over me. Thoughts of war drifted, replaced with curiosity, and I circled lower, trying to glimpse the mage.

"He's baiting you!" Ayden shouted.

A shield of ice flew over my head and slammed into the mage, knocking him over. He rose and lifted a hand. A ball of fire hovered in his palm before he let loose, but Ayden was quick and sent another shield.

Landing on the snowbank in front of the mage, I bellowed. Another stream of ice churned in my belly, soared through my throat and out of my mouth. Mages dived, some falling over the edge, screaming as they fell to their deaths.

No mercy. For that was how it had been for me. A child who lost everything. Even though the mages weren't responsible for what happened to me, they were responsible for what happened to other women and children. They needed to stare into the eyes of fierce danger and understand what they did was wrong and could never happen again.

Golden eyes turned on me, and that's when I realized the mage with the staff was King Adler.

My anger faded and unease clutched at me, for the king had come to seek me, to hunt me down because he desired my power. Now he gazed up at me with a similar expression that Ayden held. Admiration and awe. Knowing he'd captured my attention, he lowered his hands, showing me he would not use his power against me.

"I saw you in a vision." The wind blew his words to me. "You are the epitome of strength and beauty. With you at our helm, no one will stand against the mages, not anymore, and you will have everything you dreamed of. Whatever you desire is in my power to give you. Forget about the cold mountains and the ice lords, forget about the people of Lansing Falls. They are nothing compared to what we could be together. We will go forth and conqueror, make the empire of Nomadia our own. You don't have to be up here, alone. Your kind is gone, dead, but you don't have to suffer without them, when you can be great."

His words ignited something within and I was dimly aware of Ayden sliding off my back. Snarling, I changed. This time it was as easy as blinking. There came a slight discomfort and then I was back in my own body, no, my other form.

Despite the sudden shift, the fire of anger and rage kept me warm against the cold. I strode toward the mage king who stood alone, deserted by his mages. He drew himself taller, eyes widening just the slightest bit.

I sensed Ayden behind me, readying himself in case the mage king struck me down, but this was my moment. I would not go down, especially not without a fight.

The moonlight hovered near a cloud, as though frightened to show its face and I did not blame it. I curled my fingers into fists and bit back the desire to punch the king in the face.

"My name is Solvay," I told him, "and I am the last of my people, the last of my kind. We were hunted by demutos from our homeland across the great ocean to this unknown land, a land that was supposed to be full of promise. Instead, the threat my people fled from followed us. I've discovered it doesn't matter what race or nation or allegiance people hold to, they are, after all, people. They deserve the ability to live free from tyranny, without the fear of death or loss or a great sorrow, because they did not please the deities that ruled over them. And you, King Adler, are the worst of them all, because your people demand a tithe to protect the villages from the ice lords and other wild creatures. But the villages don't need protection from them, they need protection from you."

Eyes flashing I stepped closer to him, my voice soaring. "You take the women and children without regard for their feelings and mistreat them in your halls under the name of power. You use magic as shields to hide your foul deeds and to keep the people in line, using disobedience as a reason to spill precious blood. Your actions have far-reaching consequences. I tell you now, your people have caused enough death and misery and sorrow here. The ice lords starve up here in their mountains, mining precious jewels that are worth nothing if they cannot trade, while the people of Lansing Falls live in fear that you will take their loved ones, never to be seen again. You are going to leave this land, you are going to give back people you have stolen, the tithe shall be no more and we shall live in freedom."

I stopped to catch my breath while my body trembled from my speech.

King Adler stared at me, eyes gleaming as his lips curled back into a sneer. "You might be an ice dragon, but you have no authority over me or my people. We are mages, we bend magic to our ways and we will not leave, not when everything we want is here." He pointed at me. "We have sought the world for you, asked the seers, used our knowledge to divine the future. If you think we will up and leave because you are angry and believe our actions to be misguided, you are wrong. We always fight for what we believe in, and we won't stop now."

"You will." My anger rose. "Or I will come to your halls and burn them all to the ground. You've seen my other form and what I can do. I will not relent, so if you want to start this war, I will carry through."

"She's right." Ayden stepped forward. "You don't remember me, but we were raised together. I've never forgotten you, Adler, and what you did. My fight is with you, and I know your weakness. Magic may shift, and you might understand it better, but don't forget I'm an ice mage and you, you're a fire mage. Don't forget what happened when we were ten."

King Adler's eyes flashed, and he lifted a hand. A wave of fire rose. I stepped back while Ayden stepped forward, sending shards of ice racing through the air and pouring down on the fire.

I sensed there was more between the two, a history I was not privy to, and this was their fight, one of the reasons Ayden wanted revenge. I let them duel, watched them battle with ice and fire. It was beautiful, the magic dancing through the air, embers and ice shimmering in the moonlight.

They came as though called by magic. The cry of ice birds, the thump of frost giants, the shrieks of the undead as shapes formed and came, taking sides, fighting against each other. I stepped back into the shadows, leaned against the rock and took a deep breath.

Another memory struck me, my mother telling me a bedtime story. I was young at the time, six or seven, and she spoke of the creatures who took flight. Ice Dragons. Their power was great, they ruled the skies and the ground, and when they opened their mouths, they could unleash death or use fear to encourage those around them to dwell in peace. The mistake the dragons made was using violence too much, and then it turned into something else. A darkness came, the demutos crept out of the void, and they were relentless. The dragons flew away, but they always remembered who they were and why they had destroyed themselves.

I would not let darkness rule me. Dashing toward the void, I dropped into it while my wings unfurled, catching me when I needed them. I roared while magic soared and one by one the frost giants drew back, the undead returned to their tombs and the ice birds flickered away.

When the first streaks of dawn came, the only two left standing were King Alder and Ayden.

CHAPTER 19

King Alder turned and saw he was alone. His hands came down and his body sagged under a great weight. He stumbled away, dropping his staff, and moved to the edge. Staring back at Ayden, he spread his arms, his face grim. "This is what you wanted, isn't it?"

Ayden put down his hands, waiting for King Alder to give up, to apologize and decide to leave. He turned his back, and I—still in dragon form—caught the slightest flare of magic. When he spun, a fire soared out of his hands, aimed for Ayden's heart.

A scream tore out of my throat and I charged, twisting at the last minute, my tail slamming into the side of King Alder's head. With a cry he stumbled back, arms flailing, sending fiery embers dancing through the air. But the push was too great, and he fell over the edge, into the void, his cry of utter surprise echoing between the stony walls of the mountainside.

Silence descended. My strength gave way to exhaustion, and I faded, changing from dragon-form back into human-form. Ayden lay crumbled on the ground, surrounded by charred snow and mounds of ice. Bodies of frost giants and ice birds and mages surrounded him, a concoction of death.

With a cry I ran to him, falling to my knees as he sat up. "I'm fine." He reached for me, hands sliding around my waist, pulling me firmly against him. "I ducked, his blow missed me and... You saved me."

Words welled up in my throat as I held on to him and he gently pulled me to my feet. What could I say when in fact it was he who saved me? Who made me realize who I was and who cared enough to chase me down and bring me back?

"We do well together, Solvay." His arms were still around my waist and his eyes searched mine as our foreheads met. "You lent me your strength, and I used magic like I've never used it before."

I nodded, hands on his shirt, holding on, afraid if I let go, I'd be lost again. "I know what happened to my people," I told him. "The demutos followed us across the waters and lay in wait, waiting until we were comfortable and had let down our guard before striking again. It is true, the medicine kept me from changing into a dragon, but it also kept me from turning into a demuto. When I found my wings, I tried to save them but it was too late."

The pads of his fingers caressed my cheek, and I lifted my face to his touch. "Today you succeeded."

"Only with your help. If not for you, I would be lost."

"What now, Solvay?"

The tremor in his tone gave away his raw emotion. I

tilted my head. Desire rushed through me again. This time I knew who I was, and I didn't have to say no to my future. I did not have to run and hide and dwell in solitude. I was free.

I lifted my mouth to his and kissed him, hard. His hands tightened around my waist, pulling me closer, and a hunger I'd never known swept through me. Instead of holding back, I allowed my feelings to guide me. My fingers threaded through his blond hair and clasped at the nape of his neck, pulling him closer until his hard body pressed against mine. My skin burned where he touched me and my lips tingled. I parted my lips as he deepened the kiss, tongue thrusting, a groan coming out of my mouth. It was heaven, and I was falling, lost...

Until a rough laugh pulled me back to the present.

When the kiss ended, I felt bereft, as if a glimpse of bliss had been snatched away. Still holding me close, Ayden turned and lifted his head. I followed his gaze. Beyond on the other side of the shore were the ice fae. They were dressed for battle, war paint on their faces, axes in their hands and shields. Sunlight shone golden on their faces and they cheered us on.

Ayden groaned. "I'll never hear the end of this, and neither will you." He kissed me again, slow and tender, nipping my lips as he pulled away. "I hope you know I intend on keeping you."

Squeezing his arm, I smiled. "I'd like that."

"I want to try something." He turned to the gap, and his hold on me tightened. Snow and ice shot out of his fingers and danced in the wind before hovering over the void. It stretched and flattened into a road and continued until it arched over the void. The crystal bridge reformed itself under the guidance of Ayden's magic.

My jaw dropped. "Ayden, how?"

"I broke the bridge and intended to fix it, but there's something about you. I haven't grown weary when using magic, and that is an oddity. I think something shifted when you kissed me."

"Then I shall have to kiss you more." I nudged him.

Taking my hand in his, he stepped to the edge of the bridge. "Will you come with me to Val Ether?"

"Yes." Emotion twisted in my heart, the beauty of freedom, the crisp cool air, the glory of sunrise and the promise of something more. "It would be an honor."

CHAPTER 20

When the people of Lansing Falls tell the tale, they call it the time of miracles. For the ice lords swept down from their mountain and sailed across the waters to the kingdom of mages. They freed the children, sacrificed to the tithe, and took back the stolen brides. They drove away the mages, and those who remained set sail, fleeing their ruined kingdom. There was a feast like never before, and this time true joy and merriment echoed across the town. The ice fae and villagers mixed, hesitant at first, but as the food and wine and ale flowed, they grew bolder.

Ayden found me standing on the outskirts of the celebration, watching the dance.

"Why are you standing in the shadows?" He nudged my shoulder.

"It's where I've always stood." I glanced at him.

He still looked rugged but his hair had been washed and freshly braided, the runes on his arms were visible and he only wore one fur, slung over a shoulder. My heart skipped as he took his hand in mine, my skin warming at his touch.

"You don't belong on the outskirts anymore. You're one of us now, come, dance."

I smiled as he pulled me into the circle. The dancers whirled around us; the music stirred my blood, a cool breeze blew. When I wrapped my arms around Ayden's neck, my heart was full, for this was the beginning of everything.

Don't miss the next STOLEN BRIDES OF THE FAE book!

COLLECT THE ENTIRE STOLEN BRIDES
OF THE FAE SERIES!

Read these books in any order for swoon-worthy romance,
heart-stopping adventure, and guaranteed happily-ever-afters!

You can find them all at www.stolenbrides.com

JOIN NOW

Join my email list for updates, previews, giveaways, and new release notifications. Join now: www.angelajford.com/signup

ABOUT THE AUTHOR

Angela J. Ford is a bestselling author who writes epic fantasy and steamy fantasy romance with vivid worlds, gray characters and endings you just can't guess. She has written and published over 20 books.

She enjoys traveling, hiking, and playing World of Warcraft with her husband. First and foremost, Angela is a reader and can often be found with her nose in a book.

Aside from writing she enjoys the challenge of working with marketing technology and builds websites for authors.

If you happen to be in Nashville, you'll most likely find her enjoying a white chocolate mocha and daydreaming about her next book.

Tower Knights

*Gothic-inspired adult steamy fantasy romance. Each novel can be
read as a stand-alone and features a different couple.*

Gods & Goddesses of Labraid

*A warrior princess with a dire future embarks on a perilous quest to
regain her fallen kingdom.*

Lore of Nomadia Trilogy

*The story of an alluring nymph, a curious librarian, a renowned
hunter and a mad sorceress as they seek to save—or destroy—the
empire of Nomadia.*